a young boy and his best friend, the universe

Vol. I, II and III

The Good Universe Series

SAMEER KOCHURE

B19, Sangam CHS, Sai Baba Road,

Off SV Road, Santacruz West,

Mumbai - 54, India.

Publisher's Note: This is a work of fiction. Names, characters, places, concepts, and ideas are a product of the author's imagination. Locales and public names are sometimes used for atmospheric purposes. Any resemblance to actual people, living or dead, or to businesses, companies, events, institutions, or locales is completely coincidental.

Author photo by Ahsan Ali.

Vol. I, II and III cover photos by Eberhard Grossgasteiger.

A Young Boy And His Best Friend, The Universe. Boxset 1 - Vol. I, Vol. II and Vol. III/ Sameer Kochure / First Edition / Paperback

Written and Published by Sameer Kochure.

ISBN 9789354938399

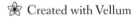 Created with Vellum

PRAISE FOR SAMEER KOCHURE'S BOOKS

A soothing read... it instantly puts a smile on your face! :)

Very cute and same time educating book. I recommend it to everyone... if you had a bad day or a good one.

And all of a sudden, the memory of my loved ones flashed back. The story went straight to my heart.

Very nice collection of stories about big questions of life, presented in a very delightful and easy to consume way. I would definitely give it to my teenager kids to read it as well!

Sameer has distilled the "WISDOM OF THE MASTERS" in just about 100 pages... It is as if the message is for you as you needed it, at this point of time... Please read this book to evolve spiritually. This book will make you happy.

A light insightful read into every human mind. The book connects to the child in everyone and answers the issues faced by every adult. A must have on every kindle for the days when child like wonder is needed the most.

This was a wonderful spiritual story about the friendship between a young boy and the universe. A story about how to think differently than you might at this time and how to appreciate what is around you. It may answer some of your questions, ease your fears or make you look at life differently, no matter what situations arise.

CONTENTS

BOOK 2 | A YOUNG BOY AND HIS BEST FRIEND, THE UNIVERSE. VOL. II

BOOK 3 | A YOUNG BOY AND HIS BEST FRIEND, THE UNIVERSE. VOL. I

ABOUT THIS EDITION

Welcome to the deluxe omnibus edition featuring the first three books in the much adored book series 'A Young Boy And His Best Friend, The Universe'.

A quick note on the reading order before you get to the good stuff. The first book in the series, Vol. III, was published in March, 2017. It was followed by Vol. II in July, 2017 and then came Vol. I in November, 2017. So, they are presented here in the same order.

However, the beauty of this book is you can flip it open to any random chapter and start reading. Chances are, that's the adventure you needed at that precise moment in your life. A happy co-incidence? Or the Universe reaching out to you with love? You decide.

A YOUNG BOY

and his best friend,

THE UNIVERSE

Vol. III

SAMEER KOCHURE

A YOUNG BOY
and his best friend,
THE UNIVERSE

Vol. III

The Good Universe Series

SAMEER KOCHURE

When I start telling a story,
I don't know what shape it is going to take.
I am as much surprised as you are...
This story is not the story I have heard before.

– Osho.

This book is dedicated,
as is everything in my life,
to my first best friend,
my Aai,
Sunanda Pramod Kochure.
All the bad in me is of my own making.
The little good in me, it's all her.

PROLOGUE

"So, what do you want?"
the Universe asked.
"Everything."
the young boy replied.
The Universe smiled and said,
"So be it."

FOREWORD

The young boy in this story is me. I have seen many moons, but I believe the young boy from our story is somewhere around six years old. As you will soon discover from his adventures, it's impossible to truly account for his age. Like most things in life, it's not important to know, anyway.

Besides, when you and I were 6, life was simple. The world was full of wonder. The best times lay in the present, not in the days ahead. We had lots of questions, and we had answers to everything.

Today, the grownups are so grown up, so restless. They don't seem to have many answers. The wisdom of innocence is carefully kept some place and forgotten. Sure, they can tell you the ideal body fat percentage, the distance to the nearest asteroid or why the economy fluctuates. But they are often found wanting for the answers that matter.

How wonderful would it be to know that every situation, every doubt, every uncertainty has a solution? How wonderful would it be to have a trusted friend by your side who could provide an answer as soon as a question arose in your heart?

That is the intent and the purpose of this book.

It attempts to answer some important questions. As you read it, don't be too surprised if you find the young boy asking a question or two that has often kept you up at night. Because while it carries my name, this book has been co-written along with the Universe.

When I was starting my working life a decade and a half ago, I had many desires, many wants and little else. That was the time I first met my friend, the Universe. I wrote a small piece that you read on the previous page. It was something that came to me, and I put it on the first page of my dream book. I even posted it on a hobby blog that I ran back then. I love it because it speaks of limitless possibilities. Till date, it has gone on the first page of every dream book I have made since.

And that's where it has rested, dormant, waiting.

Then one fine day, a few months ago, after a round of meditation, I felt a powerful urge to expand on that premise. To discover more adventures of these two best friends. And to help them find their way to as many people as possible. I put aside another book I was working on then and started writing this one. I chose to follow my intuition. It has always helped me. And I hope these adventures help you too. If by no other means, then at least, by making you smile like you did when you were a child.

As you read the following adventures, some of the young boy's questions may appear too mature for his age. Because they are not really his questions. They are yours.

I am just a channel between the Universe and you. A bridge the Universe chose to reach you. Because in truth, the young boy from these adventures is you.

And your best friend, the Universe, can't wait to meet you.

Sameer Kochure.
12th March 2017.

HAPPINESS

"*I* dropped my ice cream in the park," the young boy said with a long face.

"Oh, that's great!" the Universe chirped.

"Great?! Why is that great?"

"You just gifted ice cream to ants!"

The young boy broke into a peal of laughter, "Hahaha... gifted ice cream to ants?! What a funny thought... Hahahaha...."

"I bet all the ants are relishing it right now and thanking you for the treat."

The young boy said between laughs, "You know, happiness is an attitude."

The Universe smiled.

NOTHING CAN EXIST...

"*T*he whole world seems to be zipping past... and I am stuck in slow motion," the young boy said, "How can I get things faster?"

"Faster than who?" the Universe replied, "It's all you buddy. There is no one else in the world but you. When you look into someone's eyes, I mean really look, you'll only find yourself and nothingness. That's what you are."

"I am nothing?"

The Universe continued, ignoring the young boy's question, "When you realise that nothing can exist without you, you realise that it is all yours, anyway. It exists because of you, for you. Don't let appearances deceive you."

"Hmm..." the young boy said thoughtfully.

"By the way, you are on my side of the bench," the Universe said with a wink.

THE RICHEST MAN ON EARTH

*T*he young boy declared, "I want to be the richest man on Earth!"

"May I ask why?" the Universe asked.

"I want to have more money than anyone else in the world."

"So, if I give everyone only 99 cents, and give you a dollar, that's fine?"

"No! What will I do with just a dollar?" the young boy quipped.

"But that makes you the richest man in the world. I thought that's what you wanted."

"No... I mean, lots and lots of money so I can do what I want, when I want."

"Like travel the world, live in exotic places,

experience nice things... is that what you mean?" the Universe asked.

"Yeah, that."

"You don't need a lot of money to do that! Lots of people do that every day for very little money. Most people don't realise that they need a lot less money than they think they do. Besides, money is always provided when it is really needed. Unless people themselves choose poverty. People exercise their free will in the strangest ways."

"So, being the richest man is not a great plan?" the young boy asked.

"I reckon not, happiness is inexpensive," the Universe replied. "Besides, why aim for being the richest, when your money can be taken away any moment, by various creative fears you invented? Instead, why not focus on being the most loving person? The kindest or the most giving person? Someone who shares the most happiness in his lifetime. Now, that can go on till eternity."

The young boy said thoughtfully, "Yeah, I will be one of them. I will decide exactly which one after I finish my candy."

The Universe smiled and mumbled, "Free will... what was I thinking?"

QUIRKS AND KINKS

"*I*f all men are created equal, why do only I get a crooked nose?" the young boy asked, staring into the pond.

"It would be awfully hard for me to find you, if all of you had the same nose now, wouldn't it?" the Universe replied, "Imagine what would happen at Passport control?!"

The young boy smiled.

"You all are same, and that's precisely why I made you appear different. You may have a dozen pants in your wardrobe, but even for the same coloured denims, you know which is which by their individual quirks and kinks. That's what makes them beautiful. If humans were different from within, I would have kept you as different as a Tiger and a mouse," the Universe replied.

"Rrroaarrr...!" clawed the little cub.

THE ONE

"*I* think I am falling in love... can't be sure. Also, I don't know if she's the one for me... how can I know for certain?" the young boy asked.

"You may live a thousand lives and die a million deaths before you can know what love is... I'm not sure I completely understand it too, and I'm the Universe!"

"Then I'll never know?" the young boy asked.

"Tell me, why is knowing so important to you?"

"Well, how will I know if it is true love or not then?" the young boy asked.

"Love requires no knowing. Feel it. Your soul knows what true love feels like. It's like knowing something that was a stranger to you, as it lay hidden deep in your heart. Something that you thought was too vulnerable to survive in your perceived reality. Yet, when you meet it, you will discover that true love has a power beyond anything you will ever know. And its power depends not on the consequence or realisation of that love, but in its existence itself," the Universe said, ruffling the young boy's hair.

The young boy struck a pose and said, "I feel powerful, like a superhero."

A CLOUDY DAY

*T*he young boy said, "Sometimes I feel there is no point to it all. I just want to end everything... for good."

The skies were dark.

"Hmm... tell me, have you ever received a gift that was shabbily packed?" the Universe asked.

"Yeah... on my last birthday."

"Well, life is like that. Sometimes on the surface, it may feel like you have been handed a pretty lousy one. But it is a gift, nonetheless. Look beyond the appearances, and you'll discover treasure inside. It may take some time for you to realise just how precious it is. But would you ever throw away a present without even opening it, just because it looks shabby?"

'Never! What if there are rollerblades inside and

the one who got it for me didn't have the time to wrap it nicely and had to rush to the party?" the young boy replied.

"Exactly. Same is with life. Maybe the one who wrapped it up for you was also running late. Maybe he spent so much time looking for a priceless one for you, that there was no time left for fancy packaging."

"Hmm..," the young boy thought about it for a while.

The Universe asked gently, "It's better to allow the time for the gift to reveal itself, right?"

"Yeah! Maybe there are rollerblades AND a spaceship inside!!" the young boy's eyes lit up.

The clouds thundered, and the rain came crashing down.

"Paper boats time?" the Universe suggested.

The young boy smiled and started looking for an old newspaper.

THE INVENTION OF LACK

"Some days I feel really poor," the young boy said, "My parents work very hard... but we don't seem to have much. They do their best, so why should we suffer?"

"My child, they may be poor in money," the Universe replied, "but I didn't create lack, you guys did. What I created was the Sun, the moon, and the stars. Pretty much everything in the Universe. And there's an abundance of it available for all. No matter how poor you may be, you have a sunrise fit for kings every day. A breeze to relax the weariest of bones. Waves of the oceans to calm nerves and soil to build the biggest forests or castles. You are all rich. I didn't invent poverty or lack, you humans did. When you bring the same sense of abundance that exists in everything to money, you'll realise that there is plenty of it available for you too. You can have limitless money when you realise it's just energy. Hold it lightly and not like a miser who clutches his palms shut. You can never hold on to a sunrise and make it stay a second longer. Same applies to money. And like sunrise, it will return, once you accept the inevitability of it."

The young boy said, "Limitless, I like that."

"Yes... by the way, no one ever caught a sunrise, locked up at home, doing nothing," the Universe said with a never ending smile.

WHO'S GOT YOUR BACK

"Should I make my classmate my best friend?" the young boy enquired.

"Why do you ask? I always thought that kind of friendship just happens, no?" the Universe asked.

"Well, he is nice, quite sweet actually. Although, he doesn't let me ride his bicycle..." the young boy replied thoughtfully.

Shocked, the Universe said, "Any friend who doesn't let you ride his bicycle cannot be your best friend. There is a specific rule about it."

"Well, it seems a little harsh," the young boy replied.

"He won't let you ride his bicycle because he likes it more than he likes you. Tomorrow if you and his bicycle both are about to fall into a ditch, guess which one will he save first?"

"His bicycle... Wow, you really saved me," the young boy said, "What would I ever do without you Universe?"

"Fall into the ditch," the Universe replied, laughing like a fool.

A GIFT FOR EVERYONE

The young boy came running enthusiastically. Breathless, he declared, "I am going to give a gift to everyone I see!"

"That's a nice intent. But what can you possibly give anyone?" the Universe asked, "...even the poor have poverty. You don't even have full pants!"

"So what? I am going to gift a smile to everyone I see."

The Universe smiled with a touch of pride and said, "Now, that's wonderful. Everyone could use a smile... By the way, when you give such a priceless gift to everyone, I think it makes you the richest boy in the Universe."

The young boy gave the Universe his toothiest smile.

DO WHAT THEY DO

"Why can't my parents get along? They are arguing again... they keep arguing all the time..." the young boy said helplessly.

The Universe said, "Maybe, they don't know they are fighting... maybe they think they both are right... maybe they have real reasons to fight... maybe they are working hard but not getting ahead... maybe they had a bad sandwich for lunch, or maybe they are just hungry... I don't know exactly why they fight. However, I know a reason they are definitely not fighting for..."

"What is that?" the young boy asked with a heavy voice.

"You. Whatever their reasons for bitterness, you

didn't cause it. People do what they do because of who they are, not because of anything you did or didn't do," the Universe continued, "It's not your fault."

The young boy hugged the Universe and wept.

BLUEPRINT FOR ROCKS

"**S**ometimes I feel I am working so hard, but I'm not getting much done. Why is that?" the young boy asked.

"You mean in school?" the Universe asked.

"Nah... in life." the young boy observed.

"But you are. Don't you see?" the Universe asked.

"No... in fact, it often feels like I am going in reverse direction. I mean, look at my bank balance!" the young boy said.

"Yeah, your coin box has been pretty light of late... maybe you are not being cute enough around grandma for her to hand you that odd dollar," the Universe said.

"What nonsense! I'm adorable all the time. It's hard work, but a boy's gotta do what he's gotta do."

"Well then, I must ask you, are you doing all you

can, to have what you want? Doing your best to be at the right place, at the right time? Doing what you must in enough measure, to produce value worthy of results?"

"I think so... I am not sure."

"If you are not sure, then there's definitely scope for more. Do more, you'll have more. Don't sit around trying to get everything perfect before you begin. If I had done that, I would still have been perfecting the blueprint for rocks."

The young boy laughed and rolled up his short sleeves.

A NEW SYSTEM

"*I*s it true that there's one perfect friend for me? Someone I have to find and then I will be happy with her all my life?" the young boy asked, "... like the princes and princesses do in my books."

"Actually, those books are really old." the Universe replied.

"So, no one special person for me anymore?" the young boy seemed disappointed.

"That was the old system. Lots of boys and girls kept getting lost or missing each other and kept going around in search for years, decades and sometimes lifetimes before finding each other."

"Boy, that sounds awful."

"Yeah, it was quite frustrating to watch, actually. So I upgraded the system. I have filled the entire world with many of your perfect princes and princesses from various lifetimes. So wherever you are and whoever you find during your first, second or your nth attempt, we call him/her your prince/princess for this lifetime. Saves a lot of time and heartache."

"I like this new system. So I'll meet my princess for sure from one of my lifetimes, and she'll be my princess for this lifetime?"

"That's right," the Universe replied.

"I hope, I find the one who likes to play hide and seek too," the young boy said and ran away.

The Universe scribbled something on a Post-it note.

AN ANGEL

"*A*m I an Angel?" the young boy asked.

"No. You are something angels dream of becoming," the Universe replied.

"What is that?" the young boy asked.

"You are a human being. That's a rare and one of the most sought of honours... to be truly human."

The young boy declared, "Well then, I am going to be a mighty good one."

The Universe whispered, "And that's why you made the cut."

WANT VS. HAVE

"Can I really have what I want?" the young boy asked.

"Of course not," the Universe replied.

"Huh? I thought you would say, yes, definitely! That's what friends are for right?"

"I would rather tell you the truth."

"So I can't have what I really want?"

"Just want, no," the Universe replied, "Unless your desire is so strong that every cell of your body craves for it. Unless you will go after it with all you got within you. And, this is what most people struggle with - make room for it and accept it in your life. Once you see yourself enjoying life after having achieved it, once you start visualising that final outcome, there is nothing you cannot have. Everyone merely wants. Having it takes a little more. And yet, I deliberately kept it easy and doable for all," the Universe finished with a smile.

"You aren't my friend," the young boy said, "You are my best friend."

THE STORIES WE TELL

"*I*t's never going to happen," the young boy said.

"What's never going to happen?" the Universe asked.

"Me winning the running competition. I want to win, but the other grade students are bigger and stronger than me."

"Ah... nice story."

"I am not telling you a story," the young boy said, a tad irritated.

"Oh, it is a story alright," the Universe continued, "Everything you said after 'I want to win but...' is nothing but a story. Usually the word 'but' is a good sign that a story is about to begin. And stories are fiction. Stuff we make up."

"So you think I am making it all up?" the young boy said, shaking his head in dismay, "You should see those tall boys with long legs... how fast they run."

"Nice! You are building characters in the story; it helps it seem more real."

"Fine genius!" the young boy said, "If you know everything, why don't you finish the story?"

"A young boy wanted to win the race," the Universe continued, "The boys around him looked bigger and stronger, but our hero decided to run as fast as the wind. Try the other, bigger boys did, but our hero won, without breaking a sweat. The young boy won the actual race on the track a long time after he first won it in his mind."

"I like that story!" the young boy exclaimed.

"Guess which story will help you win, mine or yours?" the Universe asked.

The young boy said, "Yours. If I must tell a story to myself, why not tell the one that helps me?"

The Universe smiled.

NEVER ALONE

"When is it okay to cry?" the young boy asked.

"Whenever you feel like," the Universe replied, "But if you can choose, there's a time better suited to crying."

"What time is that?" the young boy asked.

"Whenever a friend's shoulder is nearby," the Universe said, pulling the young boy closer to him.

The young boy rested his head as a tear escaped him.

"Ice cream?" the Universe asked gently.

TWO CRAZY MONKEYS

"*I* have been invited to a dance party for my friend's birthday," the young boy said with a long face.

"That's great!" the Universe said, "Why do you sound so sad about it?"

"Because I can't dance. I think I'm going to decline the invitation politely, tell my friend I have to look after my parents or something."

"Whoa!" the Universe exclaimed. "Rule 1, you never say no to a party that has cake. Rule 2, you always dance."

"But I can't!"

"So what? If you wait to know something well before doing it, you'll never get anything done. Let me tell you a Jedi Master trick to dancing. Whenever you are on the dance floor and don't know any steps, or are getting too conscious, just think of any animal or a bird. Then imagine how it would move to this particular beat, and then just do it."

The young boy broke into a peal of laughter.

"Tell me if you don't win the Best Dancer prize, then!"

"Alright, I'm going... and I'm taking you with me," the young boy declared.

Then, without any music playing, there were two crazy monkeys in the room.

WHY WAIT?

"What's the best thing that can happen to us after we die?" the young boy asked.

The Universe said, "Forgiveness and understanding."

"Why is that the best thing of all?"

"Because," the Universe replied, "that's all it takes for love to blossom."

"Well then, why wait to die? Better to forgive and understand everyone, and ourselves, now only, right?"

"Absolutely," the Universe replied as they jumped on the trampoline, trying to do a somersault midair.

BONDED BY FIGHTS

"*I* don't like my brother. He is such an ass!" the young boy said, fuming.

"What did you two do now?" the Universe asked.

"He has so many nice clothes... And I have to wear the same school uniform every single day! I wish he would just..."

"Now, don't say that. Your sibling is your greatest gift from your parents."

"Oh please! Not mine!" the young boy snapped.

"Yours too, actually," the Universe said. "As you go through life, you'll find some dear friends, your soulmate. You'll share some truly great times with them and also some disagreements and fights in between. However, you may not always have your parents, friends or your soulmate around. Life can be unpredictable. You may lose them some day, or they may go away and not be around for you to fight with anymore. Then you'll miss fighting with someone whom you know you love, despite the fights. That's when you will realise the true value of having a sibling. Just to have someone to fight with all your life knowing that no amount of fights will ever lessen the love you carry for each other in your heart. Now, that's a rare treasure."

"You know, my brother is still an ass... But he's alright," the young boy said wiping away a tear.

A LOVE LESS ORDINARY

"What is love?" the young boy asked, "... what I feel for mom?"

"Yeah, maybe," the Universe replied. "Although I know something that is most definitely love, without any doubts whatsoever."

"What is that?"

The Universe said, "What your mom feels for you."

THE PURPOSE OF OUR LIVES

"What's the purpose of our lives?" the young boy asked.

"To have fun," replied the Universe without missing a beat.

"Really, you sure???" the young boy looked surprised.

"Nope. But it's a great way to keep busy until your purpose finds you," the Universe replied.

"Okay then," the young boy said playfully, "...let's get busy."

NOTHING TO LOSE

"Why do bad things happen to good people?" the young boy asked.

"They don't," the Universe replied.

"Oh, come on, someone breaks a leg, loses a house or a job... or horror of horrors... drops his ice cream. That's definitely bad."

"In the bigger scheme of things, what you consider bad always leads to something better," the Universe continued, "You lose a house and discover the entire planet is your home. You lose a job or your money and realise that you brought nothing to this planet with you, so what have you got to lose? And if you drop your ice cream, your mom gives you hers, and without realising it, your soul knows on a subconscious level that there are things and situations that may come and go in your life, but love will always find a way to sneak into your life and take care of you, again, and again, and again."

The Universe offered his ice cream to the young boy, who grabbed it with delight.

ATTACHMENT

"Why aren't all prayers answered?" the young boy asked.

"They are. Every single one of them," the Universe replied. "Sometimes though, you are so attached to hearing the answer you want to hear that you fail to hear the even better-suited answer you receive," the Universe said.

"I'm gonna keep my ears open all the time," the young boy said, pulling on his ears to be sure.

"When is giving up, okay?" the young boy asked.

The Universe replied, "Never."

Feet aching, the young boy resumed jumping. The cookie jar would eventually have to give up. The young boy just wouldn't.

LIKE A KING

"**W**hat's the best way to pray?"

"With all of your heart, of course. And pray not as a beggar who has nothing," the Universe said, "Pray like a King who has everything, most precious of all humility and a heart full of gratitude. Express gratitude for all you have and express gratitude in advance for having received that which you seek. And then, go and live like you already have it. And soon, you will," the Universe replied.

"Seems like a lot of work for a double scoop sundae, but whatever works," replied the young boy seriously.

NOT A CHOICE

"hy aren't animals smart like humans?" the young boy asked.

"Well, they had a choice to be smart. They chose to love everyone instead," the Universe replied.

"What do you mean?"

"It was an either or situation for them. They chose kindly. For humans, that is not a choice, yet most of them live like it so."

"When I grow up, I want to be a monkey then," the young boy decided.

NOTHING

"What's the absolute worst thing to do when you don't know what to do?" the young boy asked.

"Nothing," replied the Universe. "Inaction is not a sign of growth. Anything that is not growing is dying."

"Okay, and what's the best thing to do when you don't know what to do?" the young boy asked.

"Nothing. Till a better course is revealed," the Universe replied, "However, once a course of action is revealed to you, once intuition strikes, once an opportunity presents itself, once the moment arrives or something or someone catches your heart, then acting on that path, stepping forward, making your move and doing what it takes, is the only best thing to do. The world belongs to the doers."

The young boy nodded and rolled up his sleeves.

A MATTER OF PERSPECTIVE

"What would say is the best thing about this world?" the young boy asked.

"I would have to ask what is not?" the Universe replied, looking completely perplexed by the absurd question.

The young boy smiled. He didn't have an answer to that question too.

LIMITED AND LIMITLESS

"hat's the best thing I can ever give to someone?" the young boy asked.

"Love and time. One, you have so little of, and one, you have in a limitless quantity. Yet, most people live like they have unlimited time and too little love to give."

"I know some of them," the young boy replied.

"Don't be one of them and you'll do just fine," the Universe replied kindly.

YOU ARE THE REASON

"When will I be as strong and powerful as you?" the young boy asked.

"Oh, you are already more powerful than me," the Universe replied.

"Hehehe... are you making fun of me? I'm so little and you are so huge!!" the young boy said, spreading his arms wide to show just how huge.

"True, but without you, I don't even exist," the Universe replied with a touch of gratitude.

NO STRINGS ATTACHED

"What's more beautiful than to love and be loved in return?" the young boy asked.

The Universe said, "To love and be unaffected if you are loved back or not."

"That's impossible," the young boy said.

"Happens every day. Love like a mother loves her child. It matters not that the child scorns, hurts or simply abandons her. In her heart, her love remains. Love without an attachment to its outcome. Cultivate that love for your own self first. Then you'll be able to love others and everything around you the same way. Till then, enjoy the journey with abandon."

"You know something," the young boy said with a thoughtful look, "Moms are awesome."

SAMEER KOCHURE

EVERYTHING ELSE IS OPTIONAL

"*H*ow will I know I have achieved success in life?" the young boy asked.

The Universe said, "When you can go to sleep satisfied and wake up with a smile. Walk with the wind at your back and peace in your heart. When you see human beings without labels and feel nothing but love for them, unconditional love for all of them, you'll know, you have made it."

"That's it???" the young boy seemed surprised.

"That's it," the Universe replied, "Everything else is optional."

"I already have that right now," the young boy said happily.

"Congrats. Don't let it fade when you grow up,"

the Universe said, "And know that what you once had as a child, you can have again."

REFLECTION

"**W**ho am I?" the young boy asked.

"When you see me, what do you see?" the Universe asked.

"I see you, the Universe, my best friend."

"Yes, and you see something else."

The young boy asked, "What?"

"A mirror," the Universe replied.

A LOVE LOST?

"What do I do if my heart aches for a loved one? The one that was taken away from me?" the young boy asked sadly.

The Universe replied, "Love them anyway. Love never gets lost. It will find its way to its destination, whether you know it or not."

And the young boy continued loving.

EXPECT TO BE DISAPPOINTED

"*W*hy is it so hard to deal with some people at times?" the young boy asked.

"It's hard because you want to be right. You want to be better than them. Yet everyone views reality from their own perspective. And they are all right, more often than not. So forget who is right, who is wrong. Forget about trying to get along with them and love them for who they are. Because everyone always does their best. And that's all they need to do. Why expect more from them? YOU expect, then YOU get disappointed when YOUR expectation is not met and then YOU blame others. It's all about you. What have they done to deserve it?"

The young boy was silent for some time. "True...,"

the young boy said, "you are too wise to be friends with someone as young as me."

The Universe replied, "Because I am so wise, I am friends with you. And young or not, I feel blessed to have you as my friend."

They smiled and did their secret best friend's handshake.

"hy do sometimes things outlast people?" the young boy asked.

"Nothing outlasts anyone, buddy. If a car breaks down on the road, the journey doesn't stop," the Universe replied, "You are all eternal beings. What you see, hear, taste or touch is an illusion. What you feel is real. What's inside you is eternal. And it will go on till eternity. So enjoy the ride. You and I are going to do this for a very long time," the Universe said, jumping into the puddle with a big splash.

The young boy followed.

FEEL GOOD

"*H*ow should one live?" the young boy asked.

The Universe replied, "By not thinking too much about it. Contrary to the popular opinion, you can grow rich, lead a healthy and a happy life by not thinking too much about it. Think less about what you want and, instead, feel and attract it in your heart. A heart full of love and happiness will find more love and happiness in the world.""And dance. That always helps," the Universe replied, while streaming the latest hit.

They both kicked off their shoes.

ONE WISH ONLY

"*H*ey buddy, could you grant me a wish? It's terribly important to me," the young boy asked.

"No promises... but let's say, I could grant you a wish. Just one, mind you... so you must choose wisely. What would you ask for?"

"To have you, my dear Universe, as my best friend, forever and ever," the young boy said.

The Universe smiled and said, "Even after all this time, your answer is still the same."

The young boy smiled, and they both walked away hand in hand.

Like they had for an eternity.

ACKNOWLEDGMENTS

Apart from my Mom, this book is dedicated to all the gifted souls that I have had the opportunity to learn from. Without naming names, which I believe is more powerful than using labels, I offer you all my deepest, heartfelt gratitude.

Some names, however, must be named.

T. Harv Eker and Robert Riopel, who helped me fulfil the 15-year-old dream of writing a book in just four months. I see you two smiling at me for keeping my Warrior's commitment to myself. Aho!

José Silva, Dr Bimol Rakshit and Burt Goldman. Thank you for helping me discover a deeper connection with my own self. The three of you are primarily responsible for the countless miracles I experience in my life every single day.

Tejal Mamaniya who, apart from being a dear friend, always points me in the right direction on my spiritual path. Thanks for keeping me on track during the first phase of this project. And thanks for helping me learn that getting it done is more important than getting it perfect.

To Eberhard Grossgasteiger, for giving me the permission to use his beautiful photographs for the cover art of my books.

To Ahsan Ali, for his love of film and making me look awesome in the author photograph.

To my family. It's not an easy task loving me or understanding my ways, but you do a fine job of it. For that, and more, I love and thank you with all of my heart, dear Tai, Dr Monica, who is one of the most loving and strongest women I know, Jay, Dr Narhari, my thoughtful brother-in-law and Hero, my nephew Hriday, who is all heart.

And I dedicate this book to you, my dear reader. Thanks for picking it up and giving it a chance. Of course, I dream of fame and fortune, but there is no greater reason for this book to exist, than to serve you.

This dedication cannot be complete without acknowledging my best friend for eternity. Thank you, Universe.

We are in this together, my friend.

With love and gratitude,
    Sameer Kochure.

An inspirational fable about living a good life.

A YOUNG BOY
and his best friend,
THE UNIVERSE
VOL. II

SAMEER KOCHURE

A YOUNG BOY
and his best friend,
THE UNIVERSE

Vol. II

The Good Universe Series

SAMEER KOCHURE

Allow things to happen naturally... the subtle cannot be forced.

    – The Wu Wei Approach.

My life,
and everything good in it,
begins with my mom,
Sunanda Pramod Kochure.
Thank you, Aai.

FOREWORD

There's a good chance you have met the young boy and the Universe before. Your paths must have crossed somewhere, and you would have recognised each other immediately. Or it may have triggered some memory, but you could never quite put your finger on it.

Perhaps you met in the first book from this series that came out in early 2017 – Same title, Vol. III. You met, became friends, and carried each other in your hearts since.

This is not one of those friendships that is easily forgotten.

For you, it will be like catching up with your dear old friends. Only after you get together, you realise how much has happened since you last met and how much you adore each other's company.

For you, I wish you have as much fun as I had sharing a few laughs and tears with these guys again.

Then again, it's very likely that this is the first book in the series that has found its way to you. For a mighty good reason, I believe without a doubt.

As it may be, introductions are in order.

The young boy from our adventures doesn't have a name. He has never felt the need for it. His age keeps fluctuating depending on the adventure he finds himself in. Kind of like how grownups act mature in front of their bosses and like grumpy old people in front of people they don't like.

That's where the similarity with grownups ends for him, though.

What makes him young is not his age, it's his innocence. Unlike most grownups, he can voice his thoughts without prejudice, malice, and censoring. And always with a kind and loving heart.

And boy, is he inquisitive... always questioning everything from the nature of reality to the colour of gums. Some of his questions are the questions that have bothered me for a long time. So in a sense, they are my questions too.

Luckily for the young boy, he knows how to get the answers he demands. And who to ask. That's where his best buddy, the Universe comes in.

Always by his side, the Universe helps the young boy navigate through life's small and big adventures. Together they play, laugh and have fun.

As you hear some of the young boy's questions, don't be too surprised if one of them cuts a little too close to your heart. The voice is his, but the questions are yours. I am just the bridge in between.

The young boy from these adventures is really you.

And your best friend, the Universe can't wait to meet you again.

Sameer Kochure.

19th July 2017.

BIG PLANS

"Good morning!" the young boy said.

"Good mo...rrrning..." the Universe replied yawning.

"So, what shall we do today?" the young boy asked.

"Let's laugh today."

And they did.

It was a great day.

YOU GOT THIS

"*I* am not doing this. No way!" the young boy announced.

"Oh, come on, don't be scared. It's not that bad," the Universe said.

"Not that bad?? Are you nuts? It's sooo high; I could break my neck. It's way too dangerous."

"We'll be alright."

"Easy for you to say. You are big. I am tiny. If something happens, you'll probably just break a leg or something. I'll lose the amazing life that I have planned for me. What will happen to my beautiful wife and three kids? Who will pay for their college? Who will play with my grandkids??" the young boy asked.

"Wife, kids, grandkids?? You got off the school bus an hour ago," the Universe said.

"All of those are my future plans. How will they live if I won't?"

"One big drama company you are. You'll be alright, come on now."

"No way." The young boy said backing in a corner.

The Universe said, "You know, it's okay to be scared. Happens to the best of us all the time. You don't 'have' to do this. But I think you'll be alright."

"I don't think so."

"Alright, since you don't have faith in your strength and power, can you do something for me instead?"

"What?"

"Have faith in me."

The Universe said, "The opposite of fear is not courage. Courage can only exist in the presence of fear. The opposite of fear is faith. Have some faith in yourself. You got this. And when having faith in yourself seems too much to handle, just have some faith in me. I am right here by your side."

The young boy took a deep breath and stepped up. Hand in hand with the Universe, he let go.

They came down screaming.

It was the best water slide ever.

THE ONLY DUTY

"**I** don't think my parents went to the Parents' School, they totally suck at being parents!" the young boy declared.

The Universe smiled and said, "There is no such thing as a 'Parents' School' buddy."

"That explains it! There should be one. How else do you expect them to carry out their duties? They don't have any training for it!"

"Want to tell me what happened?" the Universe asked gently.

"I just don't understand why my parents behave this way. It's like they don't understand me at all." The young boy continued, "I think I am not their child, maybe a lost kid of some aliens from another planet."

The Universe said, "Your parents do the best they

can at all times. They were not made to be perfect, just as you were not made to be perfect. You get to be unique. Only you get to be you in the whole wide Universe. As do your parents."

"Besides," the Universe continued, "all parents in this world have only one task. Just one 'duty' as you call it. They don't really 'have' to raise you, care for you or make you happy. Nor do they 'have' to bring you up, care for your feelings, feed or educate you. They don't 'have' to give you the right values, inspire or protect you. That's not their mission or purpose. They don't even 'have' to love you."

"Really??" the young boy asked, surprised. "So, what is it they have to do?"

The Universe replied, "They are just there to make you their child, not need them."

"That's all?"

"That's all."

The young boy pondered over it in silence.

The Universe said, "Everything else you get from them is just a bonus. Something they chose to give you."

The young boy said, "I have a lot to thank them for then."

The Universe smiled.

COTTON IN THE SKY

"Why can't I be happy all the time?" the young boy asked.

"Do you like summer?" the Universe asked.

"Yesss... love it!"

"Why?"

"Cos, summer means holidays. I can chase butterflies, lie in the grass, stare at the cotton clouds sailing past. Life is unhurried. All my friends are free to play... and there's no homework!"

"All good reasons. But do you know why you really love summer?" the Universe asked.

"I am normal...?!" the young boy replied.

"That too. But the reason you enjoy the slow life is that you have seen the busy life. You enjoy the company of friends because you have gone without friends for some time. You enjoy the clear skies because you have braved the dark ones."

"Sure, I could have made you eternally happy, that's easy. Where's the fun in that? It's boring. Only the presence of all other emotions, the roller coaster of feelings makes happiness and peace so dear to you. Sometimes you have to know what you don't want, to discover what you want. After that, having it forever in your life is simply a choice you consciously make."

"Hmmm... true," the young boy said, "Right now I choose to eat my cotton candy, lay back and watch the clouds go wherever they are going. Care to join?"

The Universe smiled and lay down on the grass next to the boy.

Cloud gazing was their thing.

"*J* am getting an electric car. You know, for the environment." The young boy said proudly.

"Plant a tree and nurture it instead," the Universe said. "Or help heal a heart with love. Or just be kind to people around you. That'll do more for the environment than any machine could. Plus, no driving tests for love and kindness."

The young boy laughed and loved some more. The world was in safe hands.

A FORGOTTEN LOVE

"Why are there animals in this world? They should all just leave. We, humans, treat them so bad."

The young boy said sobbing. He had just left the dinner table, without touching the food, after finding out for the first time how it was made.

"You know, I have often wondered the same. So one day, I asked them. You know what they said?" the Universe asked.

"What?'

"They said - we chose to stay for the humans. Not the grownups, the little ones. The love they carry for us makes it all worth it. We only wish they wouldn't forget it after they grow up."

"I won't ever," the young boy said.

Green was now his favourite colour. Specially on the dinner plate.

BUILDS UP FAST

"I don't think I am going to score good marks this term," the young boy said. "Dad's going to be super pissed if I miss my Ph.D. because of this."

"Ph.D.? You are in primary school!" the Universe was bewildered.

"You know how Dad is... he wants me to get the best grades ...like he always did."

"You are not your dad. Your dad needs to understand this. No matter what you do, you'll never be the same. So tell him to relax and assure him you'll do your best. Ask him to expect nothing else, but your best. And then, do your absolute best."

"Why can't he just get it? The pressure of his expectation slowly builds up on me?"

"He does his best to be a wonderful dad, trust me. You should also realise one more thing. You are not your dad. No matter what you do, how hard you try to be, or try to avoid being like him; you'll never be him. So relax. And release him from the pressure of your expectation of how he should be too."

The young boy let out a deep breath. He wasn't too kicked about it, but the Universe made sense.

The upcoming test didn't bother him that much anymore.

THE LIVING EULOGY

"*H*ow do you think is the best way to be remembered when you are gone?" the young boy asked.

"Being remembered with love and affection is all that matters..."

The young boy nodded.

The Universe continued, "...both, before and after you are gone."

RIGGED

"If I am playing chess with a computer, it knows every outcome of my move, even before I make it, correct?" the young boy asked.

"Correct," the Universe nodded.

"So how is this fair? The computer knows every logical step I will follow. It takes all the fun out of playing."

"It doesn't. Not everyone is always playing to win; you'll be surprised to know. And the computer, the supreme computing power that it is, rightly knows all the possible logical outcomes of the choices you could make. But you as a player have the complete freedom to devise your strategy. You make your rules, and you choose your sacrifices. Depending on what you choose to save and what you choose to let go at every moment, the entire game changes automatically. You worry the game is not interesting for you? Let me assure you it is. And it is also way more interesting for the computer than you think. It has to make infinite calculations and sometimes just stare at you dumbfounded, and sometimes simply proud, for the completely unexpected and courageous moves you make."

"The game is not rigged," the Universe continued, "you are free to play as you please and make no sacrifices too. Learn how to play, though. Then it can be a lot of fun."

"Let's play then," the young boy said.

The cry of a newborn echoed through the hospital corridor.

GET BUSY

"I think I just met the most perfect girl ever," the young boy said.

"Congrats! You don't seem too thrilled about it," the Universe replied.

"How could I be? She had to go away in just an hour. Miles and miles away. Who knows if I will ever meet her again?"

"Hmm... isn't it good to have met at least for an hour, than never?"

"Yes, but an hour is too less."

"Okay, let me ask you, before you met her, were you sitting there thinking - 'let's see what's next on my to do list for today... ah, meeting someone awesome' - were you just sitting there, doing that?"

"No."

"Then, what were you doing?"

"I was travelling, having fun, resting when tired, playing when I felt like, doing what I wanted to do..."

"Exactly. So go out and do more of it. Just like you had no clue you'll be meeting someone awesome today, I'll surprise you again."

"Yay!" the young boy hugged the Universe.

"*I* hate Spinach." the young boy said, making disgusting faces.

"OMG!" the Universe exclaimed.

"What, what happened?" the young boy asked, bewildered.

"It's the Spinach monster! On your plate."

"What??"

"The Spinach monster... I just saw him move... OMG!!"

"Are you nuts?"

"Oh no, he's growing."

"OMG, I just saw it move a little," the young boy said, excited.

"It's growing... Soon it will take over the house,

then the town, then the world...!!!" the Universe seemed to be losing it.

"The entire world full of disgusting Spinach?? No way... Eeewwww." The young boy said, "Let's destroy it."

"But it can't be destroyed. It's a very powerful monster!"

"Then what do we do?" the young boy asked, panicking.

"Only one way. We have to eat it before it gets too big to eat," the Universe suggested.

"Alright, let's start," the young boy said, quickly stuffing his mouth with big scoops.

In a few seconds, the plate was clean. Out of breath from eating too fast, the young boy looked at the Universe and said, "There was... no monster, right?"

The Universe shrugged.

The young boy said, "I am amazed at the elaborate schemes, intricate plots, and sometimes, horrible dramas you create to get me what's good for me."

The Universe smiled and with a touch of swag said, "That's how I roll."

The young boy smiled and surrendered to the puzzling ways of the Universe.

Something good always came after.

BELIEVE

"*W*hy so serious buddy?" the Universe asked.

"A young boy in my class is gone."

"Gone where, to a different school?"

"No, died. Heart attack. At his age. Can you believe it?"

"It seems hard. I know and respect how you feel," the Universe said sincerely.

"I sense you are going to say, but..."

"Yeah, being who I am, I can tell you he isn't nearly as sad as you are right now. In fact, he's quite excited and looking forward to his new role. It's going to be a smashing comeback; I can't wait to see it."

"How do I know you are not just saying that to make me feel better?" the young boy asked.

"Believe what you want. However, you should know that I have friends in high places," the Universe said, pointing up.

The young boy chose to believe.

"By the way, I almost forgot," the Universe continued, "he sends his love and a tight hug for you."

The young boy air-hugged and felt his friend's embrace.

IT'S WAITING FOR YOU

"*R*ats!" the young boy exclaimed. "I am stuck on this essay writing assignment. Don't know what to write, what to do?"

"Go to your study table, open your notebook to a fresh page, uncap your pen, and be glued to your chair. Don't write yet. Just sit there."

"How long?" the young boy asked.

"You'll know," the Universe replied.

"What if I have to pee?"

"Don't move."

"What if I have to go real bad?"

"Don't move."

"What if I just can't hold it any longer and I still don't 'know'?"

"And there's the problem why you can't write."

"What do you mean?"

"Even before you begin, you have given up. You are confident that the urge to write won't be strong enough or you won't have your answer before you even have to pee. The problem is not that you are stuck. That is never the problem."

"Then, what's my problem?"

"The problem is that you have accepted that you are stuck even before you have made a serious, non-judgmental effort. The essay is ready to be written. It has been ready for a long time. It is just testing your desire and intention to put it on paper. It's waiting for you. The only question is will it have to wait forever because you have to pee or will you get it done first, no matter what?"

"I am going straight back to my blank page," the young boy said as they both washed their hands.

The Universe smiled and played with the electric hand dryer a little longer than usual.

I'M SO DUMB RIGHT NOW

"*I* am so angry right now!" the young boy exclaimed.

"Why are you so dumb right now?" the Universe asked.

"Not dumb, I said angry," the young boy said a tad irritated.

"I heard you the first time. So tell me, what made you so dumb right now?"

"What are you on about?" the young boy asked.

"When your emotions run high, your intelligence goes down. So you are not just angry right now, you are dumb as well."

The young boy thought about it for a moment, calm finally.

The Universe continued, "Now, tell me, if you say

something or take some action when you are angry, how would it be?"

"Dumb." The young boy said thoughtfully.

"Correct. So tell me, how are you feeling right now?"

"Not so dumb, actually."

The Universe smiled. The young boy was a fast learner.

THERE IS NO TOMORROW

"*I* want to make the world a better place. Can I do it before lunch?" the young boy asked.

"Sure," the Universe replied lazily.

"How? I was afraid it might take longer than that."

"Okay, let me ask you, by when were you thinking of achieving your goal?"

"Well, in a few years, I think..." the young boy replied.

"Then you won't even be able to do it in a thousand years," the Universe declared.

"But you just said I could do it before lunch."

"Yes, I did. The only way it works is in the present, not in the future. If you want to make the world a better place tomorrow, even a million years won't be enough. But if you decide to help just one person today, just one human being, help in any way you can, the world instantly becomes a better place. Not is some unforeseen future, but right now. Today. The only change that happens is in the present. There is no tomorrow."

"Fine, I better get started then," the young boy said as he started tying his shoelaces, which was not going so well. He gave it up and marched out barefoot.

A man on a mission.

The sun didn't set that day till the world was a shade better, and the Universe, an inch taller.

THE BURGER STORE

"Why me??? I wanted the role of the King in the school play, and the teacher has cast me as a peasant. Tell me, why can't I ever have what I want??" the young boy demanded an answer.

The Universe asked, "Have you ever been to a burger place?"

"Burger store, you mean? Of course," the young boy said.

They both had trouble pronouncing 'restaurant.'

The Universe asked, "What happens there?"

"Well, we get burgers."

"Before that, when you reach the counter, what do you do?"

"I tell the lady behind the counter that I would like a burger and thank them."

"Perfect. And what happens if you ask for ice cream instead?"

"They give me an ice cream."

"And if you ask for fries?"

"I get fries."

"Exactly, this world is also like that burger store. You can have what you want, but first, ask for it."

"Darn, I never asked the teacher if I can play the King's part."

"And has it ever happened that you wanted a burger, but your mom got you an apple instead?"

"All the time!" the young boy exclaimed.

"That's cos your mom knows what is good for you. You can play and jump around so much because of those apples. So if you ask for something and don't get it, be cool. It's probably good for you and going to help you have more fun in the long run."

"Hmmm..."

"And the most important part, don't forget to do what you do at the burger place."

"What's that?" the young boy asked.

"Offer thanks in advance."

The young boy beamed and said, "Get me a burger, will you please buddy? Thanks!"

The Universe smiled. The young boy had asked for something clearly, offered thanks in advance for getting it, and was waiting in positive anticipation of receiving it any minute now.

How could the Universe refuse?

THE DEMENTOR

"What's the worst disease that can affect people?" the young boy asked, "Cancer, self-doubt, poverty?"

"None of them." The Universe replied.

"I have heard all of them are pretty scary."

The Universe said, "They can all be healed easily if you look for solutions with an open mind and add some creativity to your plans."

"Okay... then what's the biggest disease affecting humanity?"

The Universe replied, "It's 'Ifness.'"

"Ifness? Never heard of it. How can it be so big and scary if one has never heard of it?" the young boy asked.

"I don't know why no one has heard of it, maybe

because it is not life threatening and doesn't kill you directly. It just sucks out the life force out of joy."

"Like a Dementor!" the young boy exclaimed. He could find a reason to be excited, even in the most morose setting.

It was a gift.

The Universe smiled and continued, "Yes, like a Dementor. It makes you miserable, robs the joy out of your life, fills every moment with unrealistic expectation, remorse and makes you dull. The worst part is, even if it has somehow miraculously been cured, it still leaves a nasty aftertaste. And if it has hit once, it can claim you again and again. Unless you are very careful to identify it and protect yourself from it in the future."

"Wow, that sounds like the scariest disease out there," the young boy said.

"It is."

"So what are the symptoms?"

"It is the feeling that makes you think, 'I can have this IF...', 'I will forgive him, IF...', 'I'll love her IF...', etc., you get the idea. 'Ifness' takes many forms, tries to hide in various avatars in your head and your heart. Be careful to avoid it."

"And how do I detect it?"

"The biggest sign of it is limitation, and it comes

with three clues. One, you put limits on anything you are doing, thinking or asking for, without realising it. Two, you see yourself as not deserving of something you desire. Three, you subconsciously consider yourself 'unworthy' or 'not good enough yet'. These are the signs you are suffering from 'Ifness'. Sometimes you may not even know it, but if you are carrying any regret or limitation in your heart, you are suffering from it."

"That's one scary Dementor. So how do I treat it if I am already affected or make sure I never get it in the first place?"

The Universe said, "Let go of all conditions. Conditions you put for reconciliation, for your success, for forgiveness. Let go of all limitations you put on yourself. Everyone is equally awesome and equally deserving. Just like you. You are no exception. You can have what anyone in this world can have. What anyone before you has had or anyone after you will have. You are worthy."

The Universe continued, "And it is important to know that everyone is also human. Just like you. Everyone makes a mistake. Just like you. And sometimes they take a long time to realise it. They hurt you, don't meet your expectations, and don't keep their promises. Just like you. You have done all of this in the past, and you'll do more of it in the future. So will they.

You have learnt from your mistakes eventually, and so will they. They are human too."

"So, drop all 'ifs.' Drop all expectations. And it will heal you of this horrible disease."

The young boy thought about it and said, "I was going to give you half of my chocolate 'if' I liked your answer..." He broke his chocolate bar in half and continued, "but now I am going to give it to you just because I love you."

They smiled, healed.

LET'S GO!

"**W**hich is the best path to take to reach any destination?" the young boy asked.

"The planet is round, so there are no wrong roads. You'll get there, eventually. You just got to keep moving." the Universe replied, smiling.

"Thank you, now will you answer my question, o wise one...?" the young boy said. He had just discovered sarcasm.

"Hahaha... Sure. The best path to take in any situation is always the most fun one. You'll find that it is always the shortest one too," the Universe replied.

"Superb, let's find a new fun path home," the young boy said, turning his bike towards the puddle.

HAPPINESS IS NOT IN THE SPOON

"*H*ow come babies are always smiling? What do they find so funny all the time?"

"If they found the world so funny, they would laugh so hard, they would blow their diapers off!" the Universe replied, breaking into a roaring laugh.

"Hahaha... you are so silly, Universe!!" the young boy said, clutching his belly. They couldn't stop picturing babies blowing off their diapers.

After a good laugh, the young boy asked, "So tell me buddy, why do babies smile all the time?"

The Universe replied, "They smile all the time because they are so full of love and happiness. They don't need a reason to love anyone. Babies love humans, animals, even trees. They just love. They don't need a reason to be happy. A hair clip or a spoon, whatever is at hand, can make them happy. It makes them so happy because the happiness is not in the spoon, it is in them. Because they are so full of love and happiness, they find it everywhere in the world. It takes some to find some."

"Makes sense," the young boy said, "So what about others, the grownups? Why do they look so grumpy, so bored, so stressed out all the time?"

"It's because they have forgotten all about the love and happiness that is present in their hearts. They seek it all across the world, in other people, in other things, and grow frustrated, frowning all the time. If they only seek within, they'll find it easily. People think finding love and happiness in life is a big deal, well, it's not. It's all in them. People are essentially pipelines."

"Pipelines?" the young boy looked confused. He examined himself and said, "I don't look like pipes."

"Well, you are," the Universe continued, "People are just pipelines connected to the source of everything. All they need to do is open the taps they have closed off, thinking they will run out of love and happiness if they let go too much. But you have to let it flow, let it all go out to enjoy an abundance of love and happiness in your life. Only when you leave the tap open at your end, love and happiness will flow through your life. If you want to have more love and happiness in your life, open a bigger channel for it. Build a river, make way for the Ocean. The more open you are, the more it will flow through. It's that simple."

"Okay... but babies are so tiny! How can they have such big floodgates to let out so much love that even strangers smile at them and stop by to play with them? The same strangers who sometimes don't even smile at their loved ones without reason..."

"First of all, always smile when you see someone close to you. A loved one, a friend, a stranger. Why be so serious anyway? Where's the fun in that? Secondly, babies have such a strong connection to the source, because they have just renewed it and come back into the world. Their channels are wide open. And, as it so happens, the world will slowly close that gap and make it into a trickle, if you are not careful. So it's important to keep that gateway open to the source so that more can flow through. Also, it is important to know that, eventually we all go back to the source to deepen our connection to the source. That's how we all are one. We come from the same, and we return to the same. Any tree is the first tree. A tree grows from the seed, bears seeds again, and grows till infinity. That's the nature of things. The nature of us."

"So, I am a pipeline and a tree too?" the young boy asked.

"You are me too.... And don't forget you are an earthworm too," the Universe laughed.

The young boy looked at his arms and legs and exclaimed, "Hey, I even look like pipes."

They both smiled like babies.

AND... ACTION!

"*H*ow difficult is it to make a Million Dollars?" the young boy asked.

The Universe said, "A million dollars? Do you even know what you are going to do with it if you get it?"

"Not right now... When I get it, I'll figure it out."

"And that's why you find it difficult and don't have it already," the Universe replied. "Why would anyone give you something you have no idea what to do with? Making a billion dollars can be as easy as taking candy from a baby if you follow a few simple steps. Not inviting success and struggling instead is a choice you make, not a necessity."

The young boy grabbed some sketch pens, crayons,

scissors, old magazines, chart paper and went to work. The first thing he did was put a date to his dreams.

Seeing him take decisive action to reach his dreams, the Universe went to work behind the scenes.

YOU WIN WHEN YOU LOSE

"*H*i...", the young boy mumbled.

"Wow, I could hear the sadness in that voice a mile away. What's up?" the Universe asked.

"We lost. The other kindergarten class destroyed our football team."

"So, you played?" the Universe asked.

"Yes and lost."

"But you played?"

"Yes... why do you keep asking the same thing again and again?"

"Because I fail to see how you lost. You went out there to play, and you played. That's a win for me. How does it matter which team made the most goals?"

"Well, it matters. It should matter, shouldn't it?" the young boy wasn't so sure anymore.

"Why 'should' anything? Why 'must' or 'have to' anything? That was just one game. You had a good time, got to play, got some great practice that's going to help you in your future games and so much more. Why isolate the end of the game and let it define the rest of the game?"

"Now, could you have done better as a team? Certainly. But you can't turn back time, so you'll do better in the next game. Provided you keep playing. And don't miss out on the fun of 'playing' by just focusing on the 'winning.' Both are important." The Universe said while balancing the ball on the back of its neck.

The young boy knocked it off and said, "Let's play then."

ZOMBIES AMONG US

"*A*re zombies for real?" the young boy asked.

"Absolutely," replied the Universe without missing a beat.

"You sure???" the young boy looked surprised.

"Yes. They are all around us. So many of them walk around depressed, doing things they dislike, going through the motions, doing work that doesn't satisfy them, all for the sake of a better tomorrow and for an illusion called 'security,'" the Universe replied.

"Some of them have given up already and resigned to a life of mediocrity. They are the ones that tell you 'you can't have this,' 'you can't have that,' 'the world won't be fair to you...', etc. The interesting thing about these zombies is they say 'you can't have this' but what they are saying is 'they' can't have this. Don't let their reality be your reality. Else you'll be one of those zombies too..."

The young boy nodded.

The next hour they spent picking out their best zombie looks.

SELF INFLICTED

"*I* feel terrible... I have done something horrible," the young boy said.

"What did you do now, buddy?" the Universe asked kindly.

"Not now. It's been a long time. I haven't told anyone, yet."

The Universe decided to handle this delicately, like it always did.

"I guess it involved other people, in some way?"

The young boy nodded.

"And they were hurt?"

The boy's head hung low, and he nodded again. Two tiny drops fell on the floor, right next to his feet.

The Universe asked, "Can you undo it?"

The young boy's head went sideways this time. The drops on the floor were adding up.

"Can you do anything to lessen the damage?" the Universe asked.

Sideways again.

"Is there anyone affected who you can go apologise to and reconcile with?"

"No..." the young boy's voice was quivering.

"Are you willing to own up to your mistake, confess if need be, apologise and accept responsibility, no matter what the consequence to you?"

The young boy said yes and meant it.

The Universe asked further, "Given the same set of circumstances, would you do the same thing again?"

"Never, ever, ever," the young boy replied.

"Good. So in a situation like this, where the damage is done, where you cannot undo it, where affected parties are not reachable, where you own up to and regret your actions, where even a confession or an apology is impossible, where you are willing to accept the consequences, but it's humanly impossible to do anything to make it right, there are only two actions left to take."

"What? I'll do it, whatever it takes," the young boy said.

"Fine. They are both not easy, I must warn you.

The second action is to help the person or people like the ones affected by your actions and prevent them from going through it again. Or cope with the aftereffects, as it may be relevant in your case. You can choose what form your help will take. But help you must. Possible?"

"I'll do it," the young boy resolved.

"Good. The first action to take is going to be harder. Think you are up to it?"

"I'll do it, promise. No matter how hard."

"Good. The first action is to forgive yourself. You made a mistake. It's okay. You did the best you could, at the time."

The young boy started sobbing uncontrollably.

The Universe pulled him close and said, "You are only human. You are allowed a few mistakes."

The young boy let it all go.

Soon after, all was well again.

LIVE IT

"*I* was thinking, thanks to you, I know so much more than a lot of people out there. I think it gives me an unfair advantage," the young boy remarked.

"Knowing means nothing. That's just knowledge. Soup in a can or cookies in a jar sealed shut. The only way to truly know it, is to live it," the Universe stated.

"Then all I have learnt from you, I will implement," the young boy declared.

And the young boy started living it.

The Universe watched from afar and said, "that's my boy."

THE SECRET FOR GETTING ANYTHING

"What's the best way to get anything?" the young boy asked.

"Give it first. Give it in any form, any quantity, any way you can. Give, give, give and you'll get."

"Anything?"

"Anything. You'll always get back more. If you are open to receiving it, of course. Give first. Be a Super Giver."

"Want some of my ice cream?" the young boy asked with a twinkle in his eyes.

NOT A CHOICE

"What comes easy and what comes hard in life?" the young boy asked.

"Everything. That's the answer to both your questions," the Universe replied. "What you believe to be hard will be hard. What you believe to be easy will be easy."

"What about the actual difficulty of the task itself?" the young boy wanted to know.

"That doesn't matter one bit. It's all about belief. Believe and act in line with your beliefs, go after what you want with your belief, expect it to come, and it will. It's that simple. I couldn't have made it easier if I tried," the Universe explained.

"What I find hard to believe," the Universe said, "is why do people choose to believe some things are hard?"

"Because they have forgotten about their best friend... unlike me," the young boy replied, winking.

THE HAPPY ROAD

"*H*ow do I know if I am on the right track?" the young boy asked.

"Use GPS, duh..." the Universe replied.

"I mean in life. In terms of where I am heading, what I am doing, who I am with, etc. How do I know I am on the right track with all of that?" the young boy asked.

"That's just as easy as tracking your path on GPS. Do you feel happy, not just about where you are headed, but right now in this moment? If you are happy on your path right now, you are on the right track. See, there are no guarantees in this world. There is no certainty you'll reach where you are going. No guarantee you'll reach any of your destinations. Doesn't work like that. But if you are happy right now, in the pursuit, in the chase, on the road; you are on the right track. That's why there are so many possibilities and roads of happiness for everyone. If you don't like the one you are on, switch to a happy one. It's never too late."

The young boy smiled. He was on the right track.

CLAIM YOUR POWER, YOU SUPERHERO

"*I* wish I had a superpower." The young boy said jumping (or as he likes to put it, flying in the air for two secs).

They were heading back from the new Spiderman movie.

"There's one way to have a superpower in any situation," the Universe said.

"What is that?" the young boy's eyes lit up.

"Responsibility. Take responsibility in any situation, and you'll have a great power. Just like superheroes, if you take responsibility for what's not right in your world, and take massive action, you'll immediately have the superpower needed to change your world for the better. Sometimes the change will take a while, and sometimes it will be instant. Take responsibility for your present, and you'll be able to change it for the better," the Universe replied.

"Hmmm..."

The young boy stuck a pose on a bench, and in a deep voice declared, "My name is Captain Responsible. I take full responsibility for my life and everything in it. I created it. I'll keep what I love and change what can be better. I will stand strong as a Warrior amongst superheroes. This is my destiny. In my world, justice and ice cream will be free for all. Not all superheroes wear capes, some wear short pants."

There was lightning in the sky.

A new superhero was born. And immediately he had the fan following of the Universe.

WORDS ARE TOOLS

"Why do they keep telling me, don't speak bad, don't wish anyone bad, it's just words. Why am I getting grounded for it?" the young boy asked.

"Words are weapons, my dear friend." The Universe replied, "They can hurt, kill and destroy the human spirit. Or they can be tools used to uplift, empower and comfort. Words are so powerful because they are a primary creation, used to create so many other things. They have tremendous creative power."

"Use them unwisely, and they will create your prison. Say something bad about someone, and you'll forever be in their prison. Not in a prison of their making, but of your own. The one only they can release you from with their forgiveness."

"So thinking a bit before speaking is a good idea. Your choice of words creates your world. And the quality of your words determines the quality of your life."

The young boy was silent for a while. And then said, "I must have used pretty fine words to create you then."

"You sure did," the Universe smiled and said with a touch of pride.

YOU ARE A WASHING MACHINE

"*H*ow come you are always saying laugh more, love more, when the world can be such a horrible place?" the young boy said, tears streaming down his cheeks. "If that's all we were supposed to do, why would it hurt so much, why would life seem so unbearable, if all we are supposed to be is happy?"

The Universe handed the young boy a tissue and said, "Emotions change all the time. They are energy in motion. So observe your emotions flow from happiness to sadness, to happiness again, and you notice that they are just like waves of the ocean. Forever dancing and swaying from one end to the other."

"When you learn to observe this change, not as an active participant getting affected by each change of tide but as a detached witness to this spectacle, you will realise you are not the one who flows from emotion to emotion. You are the one who sits back and observes."

"That detachment will have the answers you seek and the answers to questions you have not even asked yet. It's a higher state of being. It doesn't mean you don't feel emotions, you feel them completely. You don't run away from them or suppress them, you submit to them 100%. You allow them to flow through your life. You celebrate your joys, and you celebrate your sadness. Then you'll discover the beauty, the secrets and the wisdom of both."

"Learn to observe your emotions with a relaxed detachment. Playfully go through them and stop taking them so seriously. Then you will discover the calm and bliss that comes with detachment."

"And what about these tears, how do I stop them?" the young boy asked.

"Don't restrict them," the Universe continued, "The emotion you suppress or block will block everything else in your life. Let it flow. The tears will stop when the timer stops."

"What timer?"

"The one on your front panel."

"What front panel? I don't have a front panel!" the young boy looked to be certain.

"You do, you are a washing machine."

"What??" the young boy checked his belly for the front lid.

"Yes, you are a washing machine, and the tears are just part of the wash cycle. Your heart is being washed clean. Sometimes it takes one cycle, and sometimes it takes a few more to get it as good as new again. So be patient. Let it get washed every once in a while. Go through those emotions and release them. With that release will come realisations. That's the process."

"Hmmm..." the young boy said thoughtfully.

"By the way, what happens if you forcefully stop a washing machine mid-wash?"

"Well, the dirty clothes remain dirty, swimming amidst dirty water... and they stink."

"Exactly, so it's important to complete the wash cycle and not interrupt it, else you also end up with a heart that, you know, stinks."

The young boy laughed at this. Somewhere during the conversation, the tears had stopped.

The wash cycle was complete.

THE COST OF JOY

"What's the cost of joy?" the young boy asked.

The Universe replied, "Action."

"What do you mean?"

"Joy comes from action. A physical, mental, emotional or spiritual action. Something has to move for you to experience joy."

"I never knew there is a thing called as mental, emotional or spiritual action..."

"There is. Sometimes it's about taking action in the physical realm which you are most familiar with, like an action to change your surroundings, job, financial situation, etc. There are many physical steps you can take to change that."

The Universe continued, "However, you may find

that everything in your physical realm is perfect, but joy is missing in your heart. Happens?"

The young boy nodded and said, "It has happened to me, and I know a few people like that too."

"True. For them, the action required is nonphysical. They will do well to change the focus of their energies from an elusive quest for something illusory that will give meaning to their life, to asking themselves a simple question."

"What question?" the young boy asked.

"How can I help?"

"Help...? Help who? How? When?" the young boy asked.

"Doesn't matter. Everyone with a mental, emotional or spiritual barrier to joy will have a different answer to this question. And all of those answers will be right for them. Just ask yourself the right question, 'how can I help?' And then listen for the answer that comes. Most of the times the answer will come immediately, and you will go, 'why didn't I think of it before?' Sometimes it will take a little longer. Still, if you keep your ears, mind and heart open; you will recognise it instantly. Then just follow the course of action that the answer reveals to you."

"And that action will unlock joy and purpose in my life?"

"Absolutely, 100%."

"Good to know. Actually, even chocolate unlocks joy in my life," the young boy said taking another bite of his chocolate bar.

"True. But it lasts till the chocolate bar does, right?"

The young boy said, "That's true. So tell me, how can I help?"

The Universe smiled and said, "You are already helping millions and billions of people, my friend."

The young boy smiled and said, "Then I will keep helping people forever."

The Universe smiled back and silently vowed to help the young boy forever.

ACKNOWLEDGMENTS

When I wrote and published my first book four months ago, I was on top of the moon. It was a long cherished dream that was finally realised. I have always wanted my books to be my humble gifts to the world. That was the intention, at least. And while I wrote it with that spirit, soon after it got out, a bit of ego slipped in. I was an author now.

I started telling people (who asked) that independent publishing is the way to go. 'Because I spent a month figuring out how writing, designing and getting a book out works, now I can easily get the next 40/50 done because the process is the same.'

I had forgotten humility.

As it turned out, just writing the second book proved to be a huge personal challenge. I would go to nice places just to write, open my notebook and sit. And nothing would come. I would go to beaches, cafés, try getting up early morning to write or try writing past midnight; but nothing moved. I have written my books by the process of channeling. That's why the voice of wisdom comes through strong and connects with people. I don't get in its way. It's not something I am in control of. I can make time for it, get ready for it, wait expectantly for it, but the magic depends on something else, beyond my control altogether.

I struggled. Panicked over the rapidly approaching deadline. I had given my word - I'll have this book written and released on my mom's birthday. I couldn't stop thinking, what if I don't make it? What kind of person I am if I can't keep my word? A warrior's word is law. So I kept inching forward.

Then it happened. Slowly, like a trickle at first, then it came in torrents. I wrote and wrote. Things started moving. The right help for design, formatting, ISBN, arrived on time. Soon, it was done. Right on the day, I had committed to myself.

It taught me a few valuable lessons.

I didn't do it alone. Everything I learnt until now, and the people I learnt it from, contributed to making it happen.

And therefore, this book is dedicated to all of you.

Shifu Carlton Hill, who taught me that the energies of the Universe are soft. It's best to let them take the natural course and not force them to my timetable for success. Success is a byproduct, he said. Focus on your passion, don't worry about success. I am following that advice. I don't know about success, but it makes me happy in the now. And that counts big time. Thank you, Sir.

Blair Singer, who taught me the importance of giving. 'Give, give, give first,' he said. Be open to receiving, but focus on giving first. The areas where I have already implemented his advice, including this book series, I see magic happening. Thank you, Blair.

Dr Bimol Rakshit, whose words, 'when the next step keeps getting easier and easier, you are on the right path' made me realise I am on the right track. Even when the writing was not moving, other things in my life were moving because of it. Thank you, Sir, for helping me find my path.

Tejal Mamaniya who, once again, kept believing I will meet my deadline when I was wanting in that belief. I cannot emphasise enough the importance of having people around you who believe in you. They are your angels. Thank you so much, Tejal.

Thank you, T. Harv Eker and Tim, for helping me discover my mission and live my vision.

Thank you, José Silva, and Burt Goldman, for your continued guidance and countless miracles I experience in my life every single day.

And a big thank you to my family. Dear Tai, Dr Monica, who is amazing in every way. Jay, Dr Narhari, my caring brother-in-law, and Hero, my nephew Hriday, who lives up to his name.

And a big thank you to my loving aunt Viju maushi and Uncle, Gau, Sam, Pinks, and Ishaan. Time always flies whenever I am with you guys.

To Eberhard Grossgasteiger, for giving me the permission to use his beautiful photographs for the cover art of my books.

To Ahsan Ali, for his love of film and making me look awesome in the author photograph.

And this book is dedicated to you, my dear reader. Thanks for being here. The only reason this for this book to exist is to serve you.

Lastly, this dedication goes to my best friend for eternity, the Universe.

Thank you, buddy. Let's dance and play together, forever.

With love and gratitude,
Sameer Kochure.

An inspirational fable about finding success and happiness.

A YOUNG BOY

and his best friend,

THE UNIVERSE

Vol. 1

SAMEER KOCHURE

A YOUNG BOY
and his best friend,
THE UNIVERSE

Vol. I

The Good Universe Series

SAMEER KOCHURE

Watch the Universe create through you.
It can use you to do its work.

– Shakti Gawain, Living in the Light.

To the one
who was so easy to love,
my mom,
Sunanda Pramod Kochure.
I don't know how you did it,
but you have certainly found a way
to send us, your dear ones,
love and blessings from beyond.

FOREWORD

There are two characters and a million lives in this book. Chances are you have met them all in the world out there. The young boy and his best friend live openly amongst us. They ride the same subways, watch Netflix all night, even devour the same Pizzas. So there's a good chance these two have crossed your paths somewhere, and you have met them before.

Perhaps you may have met the young boy and the Universe in volume III and II of this book series (written and published in that order, before this book). If you have been through those journeys, I am sure these crazy cool characters have made a home in your heart too.

For you, this book would be like a homecoming.

A chance to snuggle up with your loved ones by

the fireplace, hot cocoa in hand, and sharing stories of warmth while looking at each other with eyes radiating love.

To you, I wish an evening of catching up, laughter and happiness ahead.

Then again, this may be the first book in the series that has found its way to you. I am sure, for a good reason. I am a firm believer that you don't choose a book; a book chooses you.

As it may be, introductions are in order.

The young boy from our adventures doesn't have a name. He has never needed one. He could just as easily be a young girl. Read it as such, if you prefer.

His age also keeps fluctuating depending on the adventure he finds himself in. It's not his age that makes him young; it's his innocence. He speaks what he feels without judgment, and lovingly questions everything without the fear of looking silly. How many grownups do you know like that?

It's a gift, his loving, inquisitive heart.

And because he questions, he gets the answers.

From his equally crazy wise friend, the Universe. You may, just like me, find it impossible to imagine the physical appearance of these two best friends. After all, the truly important things in life are impossible to visualise. Like love.

And this is a story of love.

Always hand in hand, the Universe helps the young boy navigate through life's travesties. Together they play, laugh and have fun.

As you hear some of the young boy's questions, don't be too surprised if one of them cuts a little too close to your heart. It may be a question that has kept you up at night, once too often.

The voice may be the young boy's, but the questions are yours.

I am just a pen. The hand wielding it belongs to a higher power. A power that wants to talk to you now. It has been listening to all your questions and is trying to reach out to you with love.

The young boy from these adventures is you.

And your best friend, the Universe, can't wait to meet you again.

Sameer Kochure.

4th November 2017.

AN UNIMPORTANT THING

"*M*oney is not important, right?" the young boy asked.

"Absolutely," the Universe replied lazily. "That's why make a lot of it. After all, which wise man or smart woman would like to spend his or her precious time and mind worrying about an unimportant thing like money, or the lack of it?"

The young boy nodded, rolled up his Spider-Man t-shirt sleeves and went to work.

The Universe got its chequebook out.

SOMEONE'S BEST DAY

The young boy slammed the door shut, threw his school bag in a corner, lay down on the bed face down, and buried his head in a pillow.

The Universe said, "You seem to be having a great day!"

"Go away," the pillow said.

The Universe asked, "What happened?"

"Teacher selected class Prefect today. I wanted to be one, was working so hard for it, studying, paying attention in school, doing my homework on time, even going out of my way to keep the classroom clean. Still, the teacher picked him. He's so smart, always getting the top grades, raising hands at every question... he even has his father pick him up from school every day, while I have to take the stupid bus."

"Why can't I have all that? Why am I not like him?!" the young boy demanded.

The Universe replied, "Don't compare someone's best day with one of your bad ones. That's the problem with comparison. When everything is going well, you don't compare. When you get to sing with other kids on the bus, you don't compare. When you don't know the answer, but the teacher picks another student who doesn't know the answer as well, you don't compare. You only compare when something doesn't go right for you - according to you."

"You compare when you are already low and not having one of your best days. And who do you choose to compare yourself with? Someone who is having one of their good days. Maybe their best day. You don't know their backstory of how they got there. How many things were they deprived of before they got what you envy them for... how is that fair? Perhaps that kid was sacrificing his PlayStation time every day to study harder and score better marks. Perhaps he didn't have PlayStation."

"You can never truly know anyone's backstory. So drop all comparisons. Have faith that all will happen in good time. Often, after some time has passed, you'll discover, what you originally thought was bad eventually lead you to something nice and wonderful."

"Hmm..." the young boy hummed.

"Besides, I believe they will pick the sports captain next week, right?"

The young boy jumped with joy. "Yes! You can't be both class Prefect and sports captain at the same time. Now, I can throw in my name for that," the young boy said, dancing with the pillow on his head.

The Universe laughed.

BAD LUCK

"*I* lost my crayons..." the young boy came home crying. "They were my favourite..."

"Hahaha..." the Universe erupted in laughter.

The young boy punched the Universe in the stomach and said, "Stop laughing! This is serious business!"

"Huhuhahahaha..." the Universe bellowed.

"You are making fun of my misery?? You know how much I loved my crayons? All my important work, my homework assignments, my spaceship blueprints, everything I drew with them..."

"Hohohahahhahhaha...!" the Universe was rolling on the floor now.

"Stop it!" the young boy went on his knees beside

the Universe, urging it, pleading it to take him seriously.

The Universe was clutching its stomach as it continued to laugh, "Hohohehahaaaa..."

"Stop it..." said the young boy as a smile started to spread on his face. "I like to take my troubles seriously," the young boy protested feebly.

"Hoohohoooo...." the Universe hollered and started tickling the young boy.

"Stop it... hehehe..." the young boy managed as it joined the Universe rolling on the floor.

On his back, in between laughs, he told his best friend, "You know, a good response is the perfect antidote for bad luck."

They both continued laughing and tickling each other as the Universe beamed with pride.

LOVE AIN'T FAIR

"You are more loved than you'll ever know." The Universe answered the question the young boy had not asked.

"How is that fair?!" the young boy moaned.

"Of course, it is not fair," the Universe replied, "But think about it; in a way, it is quite wonderful."

The young boy thought about it. Then smiled through smoky eyes as the Universe drew him closer.

"*W*hy do you talk about giving all the time? Why do you say give, give, give? I am more interested in getting. Why don't you ever tell me to get more? Get more toys, more ice cream, more candies? Why this focus only on giving?" the young boy asked.

"Giving is trusting, buddy," the Universe replied. "When you give chocolates to someone, you trust that you'll have more chocolates. If you aren't willing to give to others, you'll have trouble receiving."

"Receiving is nothing but giving to your own self. When you hesitate to give to others, you hesitate to give to yourself too. If you hide chocolates in your bag and don't eat them or share them with your friends; eventually, they'll go bad. What's the point of having something that you cannot use, share or enjoy? Is it any different from not having it in the first place?"

"Whatever you hoard, you lose. Whatever you give, you get to keep. That's the law of the Universe."

"I didn't know there were laws named after you..." the young boy said wide-eyed.

The Universe laughed and continued, "I know, it's cool, right?! Anyway, that's how that law works. It's like love. The more you give, the more you'll have. That doesn't mean you should give with the expectation of getting it back. Give to give. A river carries rich soil that it has rightfully earned in its passage through the lands. Then it gives it freely to the banks along the way. And the river becomes purer for it. When it meets the ocean, it is in its purest form because it gave freely along the way. The lands are richer for it too."

"Giving is keeping things in circulation. Circulation keeps us alive. Look at your body. When blood circulates in your body, you feel alive. The deeper the air circulates in your lungs, the more tranquil you feel."

"Now think of the same blood, same air not flowing through the body. The body hoarding it out of a misguided fear of limitation, the fear that the air may run out and not return in time. What would happen to it?"

"Decay and bad breath?" the young boy ventured a guess.

The Universe laughed and said, "Much worse than bad breath. What's not in circulation is dying of stagnation. Movement is life. So stay in circulation. Whatever you wish to receive more of in life, start giving it away first. Small or big, size doesn't matter. It only matters that you give. Give it freely, with an open heart. Keep giving, to be in the natural flow of life."

"Okay, I'll start right away. Now, I give you the unique opportunity to help me with my French homework," the young boy said with a wink.

The Universe pinched the young boy's cheek and loved him even more.

THE BEST LIVES EVER

"**W**hy do some moms die so early?" the young boy asked, tears rolling down his cheeks.

"Someone had to sit on the heads of the powers that be up there, and ensure that their kids have the best lives ever," replied the Universe.

The powers up there were nudged into action and relayed a direct order to the Universe.

Following the instruction, the Universe gave the young boy a tight bear hug.

AS REAL AS IT GETS

"*D*o you even exist?" the young boy asked, "Or are you a work of my imagination?"

The Universe smiled and said, "Can you show me even one thing that is not a creation of your imagination?"

The young boy smiled.

Even at such a tender age, he had the smarts to know that his best friend was as real as the rest of the world.

VAMPIRE ANTIDOTE

The young boy looked under his bed for the nth time.

"What's up, buddy?" the Universe asked.

"I can't get sleep. I saw a trailer for a vampire movie today... Now I can't get those frightening images out of my head. Please tell me that vampires are not real."

"I would, but I would be lying then. Sadly, vampires are very real buddy. But they are not the kinds that would hide under your bed or suck your blood. The real vampires look like normal people, they don't even have fangs like the movie vampires. They hide in schools, offices, gym, among your friends, or even in your family. The actual vampires look and talk like normal people. They can even easily go out in the sun and not be burnt to ashes like the movie vampires. These vampires are very resilient."

"Really? That's scary! How do I even have a drop of blood left in my body if I am surrounded by vampires? Is my blood not sweet enough?"

"These vampires feed on something they find sweeter than your blood."

"What's that?"

"Your positivity, your joy, your happiness."

"What?? No...!" the young boy was horrified.

"Yes. These are energy vampires. Whenever you interact with them, however briefly or long, you feel exhausted and emotionally drained. Often they hide their invisible fangs behind the cloak of helping you, protecting you from the evils of the world and seem to be well meaning towards you. But that's their disguise. Often they themselves are unaware that they are energy vampires. But they drain the life force out of you and leave you feeling down and out. No matter their intention, they end up doing more damage to you than the damage they claim to be protecting you from."

"The worst kind of energy vampires make their way into your mind and hide there, instead of under your bed. That often makes them undetectable."

"That's super scary," the young boy said.

"It sure is."

"How do I know if some of them are hiding in my head?" the young boy asked, tapping his head.

"Easy. Just think of the people who, when you think of them or of what they said or did; you feel low, drained and tired. Just like they make you feel when you are interacting with them in real life. They are equally effective at draining your energy, be it in real life or in your mind."

"I know them!" the young boy exclaimed. "Some of them are even hiding in my head... I am doomed!"

"No, no. They are quite easy to get rid of, actually. More easily in your mind than in real life, anyway. But the antidote will work in real life too; it just needs a more prolonged application on your part."

"Next time you catch yourself thinking of an energy vampire, become aware of it and immediately start thinking of someone positive in your life. If you can't think of anyone, look up a video online of someone inspirational, a sports star or a scientist, an artist or an astronaut, anyone who has achieved what you desire in life, or lives the life you dream of living. Read their books, blogs, and soon your mind will fill with energy vampire destroying antidotes. You'll be safe and protected then."

"And what about the real-life energy vampires in my life?"

"Avoid spending as much time with them as possible. If that's not possible, if they are amongst your close friends or family, then create a shield around yourself with your imagination. See this invisible shield made of impenetrable light. A shield so strong that the fangs of energy vampires, or anything negative for that matter, cannot break through. Energise this shield often by simply thinking about it working and getting stronger by the day. Just this one activity done regularly will keep you protected from the energy vampires everywhere."

"And for every single one energy vampire you spot in your life, fill in at least three positive, encouraging people. Meet or talk to them whenever you feel drained. Sometimes the energy vampires work silently, and you don't realise you are down and out because of them. So you need a support system made up of positive people. Tap into your support system even when you don't need it. Your support system can also be made of books, audio, video or even comics as long as they are positive and uplifting. As long as they help you believe big things are possible for you and help you discover the greatness within you. This antidote works effectively as long as it is taken immediately after your encounter with an energy vampire. Otherwise, it takes a stronger, consistent dose of the same. Initially, you may need a heavier dose to build up your immunity. Then you'll automatically adjust to a lower dose taken at regular intervals because you never know when you'll encounter an energy vampire."

"Great. I'll start today itself." The young boy grabbed a biography from his dad's bookshelf, and heading into the bathroom, continued, "I must protect my energy."

The Universe smiled.

ROOM FOR LOVE

"*T*his guy in school is such an idiot..." the young boy started saying.

"Order! Order!!" the Universe cut him short by banging the see-saw loudly and continued with a booming voice, "The court is in session now."

"What's with you?" the young boy look puzzled.

"Go on Judge; the court is quiet and ready for you."

"What court, we are in the playroom. And what Judge?"

"You just passed judgment on someone, didn't you? That makes you our honourable Judge."

The young boy thought about it for a moment.

"But I hadn't even considered any proof, or witnesses, or given a chance to the accused to defend himself. I sentenced my friend to be an idiot straight away."

"That's right," the Universe nodded.

"I don't want to be that kind of Judge. I want to be fair, I want to give people a chance."

"Let's leave the judgments behind than, shall we?" the Universe suggested.

"The motion is passed with unanimous votes from the jury." The young judge banged the see-saw and sealed the verdict. He continued, "Judgements don't leave room for love."

The Universe smiled and cheered the decision of the playroom court.

QUESTION THE QUESTIONS

"*W*hat's more important than getting the right answer?" The young boy asked.

"Asking the right questions," the Universe replied with all seriousness.

"Only the right questions lead to the right answers."

The young boy smiled. He had asked the right question.

The Universe continued, "If you are not getting the answer that will solve your problem, ask better questions."

The young boy said, "Better questions = Better answers."

The Universe knew the young boy was a fast learner, so it threw in one more piece of the puzzle well beyond the grasp of someone so young, "And begin by asking yourself first."

"I already do that," the young boy replied.

The Universe smiled. It had been underestimating the young boy.

This boy was going places.

THERE'S AN APP FOR THAT

"*I*s it possible to go back in the past? Can you build me a time machine?" the young boy asked.

"Why do you want to go back?" The Universe asked, "Kids your age can't wait to grow up, and you want to go back. You'll be a baby again. How will you ask me questions then, when you won't even be able to talk then? Gooo... goo..." the Universe started acting like a baby and laughing at the thought.

"Stop it. I am serious." The young boy insisted. "I want to go back and change something... for the better. It's very important."

"Oh, you don't need a time machine for that. There's a program pre-installed in your head for that already. Like an app."

"Really, what app is that?"

"The kind that auto-updates."

"What is it called?"

"Imagination."

"You are kidding, right?" the young boy said, "It's not a time travelling app!"

"Of course it is. Here, let's try it. Sit quietly. Good, now close your eyes."

The young boy played along and closed his eyes.

"Think of the time you would like to go back to. If other thoughts come to distract you, just tell them gently, you are busy now and will deal with them later. Focus on that scene, the place you want to go back to."

"What time of the day is it? You should be able to see it clearly now. You can hear the sounds... smell the fragrances in the air from that time... Touch something and feel its texture. Imagine you are there, as real as it gets."

"Watch the scene you want to change from a few minutes ago. It is now playing out exactly as it did before. Imagine this scene in great detail, in full colour. Now the part you would like to change is about to begin. Before it begins, imagine all the colour from the scene fades out. Imagine the scene becoming blurry. The unpleasant part is being played, but it is out of focus, like a video file that has gone corrupt. It's unsaturated, black and white, unreal, no drama, no sounds, no smells nor life in the scene. It's like watching something that's not real, something out of place."

"Now, rewind it to a few minutes earlier. Everything leading to that part is still the same. Bright, vivid, lifelike. You are there, having the same experience leading to the event. Now as it approaches the event, this time, change the scene to what you would like to have happened. See yourself safe, protected, doing the right thing. Other people are doing the right thing too. All of this plays out in bright colours, with Ultra High Definition, IMAX quality. You can hear yourself saying the right things, others responding positively. You can smell it in the air - the feeling of all being well."

"You pick a small object and feel it in your hands. Feel its weight, the texture, the warmth or coolness of the material. With this object in your hands, look up and see the scene from a distance now. You can see yourself from a distance in that situation. Now you are not part of the scene, but a silent observer from a distance. Things are going right now. The right things are being said, the right things are being done, and the right feelings felt and expressed. The right actions are taking place in front of your eyes now. All is well in your world again."

"Now, come back to the present and gently open your eyes, whenever you feel ready."

After a few quiet moments, the young boy opened his eyes. There was peace in them.

He smiled to the Universe and touched his cheeks. Surprised, he asked, "Why am I sweating from my cheeks, the aircon is not working?"

The Universe shrugged and smiled.

"**W**hat the! I can't believe they did this...!" the young boy exclaimed.

"Who did what?" the Universe asked.

"They just ended my favourite TV show, with one of those open to interpretation endings. What's this fascination with open-ended endings? Why can't they just make it clear what happened and whether it was worth it?" the young boy asked.

"Maybe it's not the question of a better ending, but a question of better viewing, a better point of view on your part."

"What do you mean?"

"The end is what it is – an end. Why do you seek fulfilment, happiness, and meaning as a destination at the end of your journey? Why not look for it along the way? Why not make it the way? Then, the ending won't matter. You'll be happy throughout the journey."

The young boy smiled and turned his kite towards the happy skies.

HEAR IT IN EVERYTHING

"*I* love you... you know, like a friend," the young boy said.

The Universe laughed and said, "I love you too, buddy."

"Why don't you say it often then?" the young boy asked.

"I say it very often, my friend. Not with my words, but with my actions. You'll be able to hear it in everything that happens to you and around you; if you are listening."

"Always listening mode turned on," the young boy said, clicking his head.

The Universe smiled.

"**What's** so bad about expectations? Why do you keep telling me not to expect?" the young boy asked.

"The problem with expectations is that they are often misguided," the Universe replied. "You get caught up in unimportant details. You plant a seed and keep watering it every day, expecting a beautiful rose to flower. Plum, soft, delicate petals, enchanting fragrance, rosy cheeks, and whatnots."

"Yet, sometimes, what blooms is a lotus. You couldn't tell from the seed; it looked like a rose seed to you. So you don't get small, delicate petals, and you can't make a romantic gift of a lotus to a beautiful girl; so you get disappointed. You want a rose so bad; you cannot see the beauty of the lotus."

"You planted a seed in the soil, yet the attachment started growing in your heart. You feel, the flower came into existence because of you. The truth is, it came into existence through you, not because of you."

"And it flowered into what was in its heart. You thought your seed held the promise of a rose, yet it was always meant to be what it was at its core."

The young boy thought about it for a moment silently and then said, "Kind of like us children, right?"

The Universe smiled.

∽

"**W**hat is more important, actions or results?" the young boy asked.

"What's in your hands?" the Universe counter-questioned.

"Actions."

"Then, that must be the important part. Remember, the important is always in your control. And when you control the important, other bits also fall into place."

"When you act right, as guided by your inner voice, your voice of wisdom, you'll always get the right results. Sometimes you'll know immediately that the results are right for you, and sometimes it may take a little longer for you to realise that the results were for your highest good, all along."

The young boy smiled and took a small action, a quick step towards his dreams. In an instant, he was miles ahead of the ones just thinking about it.

SET YOUR MIND RIGHT

"How can I be taller than a mountain?" the young boy asked as he marked his height with a pencil behind the door.

The Universe took the pencil, went to do the same and replied, "By taking one step up the mountain and then the next, and then the next... so on, till you reach the top."

"It will take a long time for me to conquer the mountain."

"No, you'll conquer the mountain with the first step you take, after having set your mind right. The first step, after deciding to go on till you reach the top."

The young boy set his mind right and fastened his shoelaces.

PLAN FOR THE UNPLANNED

"*I* have big plans for my life ahead!" the young boy said, beaming with joy.

He showed his planner, notes, chart papers with beautiful cutouts from magazines pasted on them, colourful scribbles drawn with markers to the Universe.

The Universe smiled and said, "Thanks for providing the blueprints, most of the time I have to play guesswork with people. Invariably I get a few things wrong. An easily avoidable mistake. These plans are truly wonderful."

"You are welcome," the young boy said, going pink in the cheeks.

"By the way, I hope you left a few pages blank?" the Universe asked.

"Blank, what for?"

"Pleasant surprises. Delivering things more wonderful than you imagined or expected is my specialty, you know."

The young boy smiled and left a few pages of his planner and some parts of his colourful 'My Super-Duper-Awesome-Forever Life' vision board blank.

How he loved surprises.

EASY PEASY

"Why do you answer all my questions?" the young boy asked.

"Because you turn to me for answers," the Universe replied.

The young boy smiled and said, "I never imagined getting the right guidance was this easy."

The Universe winked and said, "Actually, you did."

"**F**rench is so difficult," the young boy said, looking up from his textbook.

"Well, you selected it as an optional language," the Universe replied.

"That's because I love French fries and I thought they would teach me how to make French fries."

"Hahahahahahaaa...." the Universe burst out laughing.

"Stop it..." the young boy said, smiling.

The Universe continued, "Hahahahaaaa.."

"How was I to know? Stop making fun of me ..." the young boy said.

"I am not... hahaha... making fun of you buddy... hahaha... I think you are..."

"I am... what?!" the young boy demanded.

Rolling on the floor, the Universe continued, "I think you are soooo adorable... I love you so much... always stay the same... hahaha..."

The young boy smiled with all his heart and joined in on the laughter.

The Universe said, "Being non-serious and playful is the way to win the world."

The world belonged to the young boy.

"We have a cleanliness drive in school tomorrow. We have to collect garbage off the streets, that's so disgusting," the young boy made a face he made when there was Spinach for dinner.

"So why are you doing it?" the Universe asked.

"To help mankind," the young boy replied.

"If you want to help humanity, that works too. But there are better ways to do that."

"Like what?"

"Dream a dream. Something nice and big and wonderful that you want for yourself. And then go out and achieve it."

"That will be nice for me. I don't see how it helps humanity?"

"The world is full of people who have stopped believing. People who doubt the possibility of their dreams ever coming true. They doubt that good things can happen to them given their situation, education, gender, age, or where they come from."

"Show them it is possible. Show them it may not be super easy, but it is not that difficult too."

"Roger that!" the young boy said with an army salute. "I'll live my dreams."

The Universe smiled and said, "So be it."

THE UNIVERSE WITHIN

"Why do so many people across the world need help?" the young boy looked tired.

"Everywhere I turn, there's someone in need. People asking donations, someone asking a friend for money, waiting for a friend to rescue them from an abusive relationship, or hoping an organisation or the government will save them from financial doom. Kids waiting for their parents to make their lives better or parents waiting for their kids to take care of them; why are so many people desperate for help?" the young boy asked.

The Universe said, "So many people are constantly asking for help because asking and waiting for help is easier than taking responsibility and helping your own self."

"But what if they don't know how to help themselves?"

"They don't know cos they don't ask themselves 'what can I do to change my situation for the better?' The truth is, there is an entire Universe within themselves that they can turn to for guidance. Everyone has that access. Few ever use it."

"It's very easy to identify the ones who tap into their own Universe of wealth and wisdom and help themselves."

"How is that?" the young boy asked.

"These are the people who are busy helping others. They are the ones with bright futures and enormous fortunes ahead."

The young boy looked at his book and said, "I don't need your help with this math problem. If you need help with yours, let me know. I am happy to help."

The Universe smiled.

WAIT A LITTLE

"*W*hy do I see so much good and bad in the world at the same time?" the young boy asked.

"That's because there is good and bad is in you too. And in everyone else on this planet."

"Then how come some people are more kind, helping and loving, if there is bad in them? And how are some people so mean, hurtful if there is good in them too?"

The Universe said, "It all depends on when you act."

"What do you mean?"

"You feel anger, jealousy, pride, and all other negative feelings, right? Similarly, you feel love, happiness, and peace, right?"

"Yeah, and I am sure everyone else does too. That's what makes us human, no?" the young boy replied.

"Absolutely. It's only natural to feel a range of emotions, thoughts, and states. Positive and negative co-exist in nature and in yourself too. What you have to carefully and consciously choose, however, is the moment when you act. If you act when the negative in you is stronger, you'll take wrong actions and justify them to yourself easily too. The truth is both positive and negative in you have tremendous power."

"I thought I was good; I didn't know I was just as easily capable of doing something bad. How do I avoid acting when the negative in me is strong?" the young boy asked.

"Thankfully, this is easy. Just be conscious and remember this step. Learn to be more patient. Always act when the positive in you is stronger. When you bring your awareness to any situation at any moment, you'll know if the positive is dominant or the negative. If you find the positive is in control, take that action. If you find the negative is in the lead, wait a little. Just a little patience and you'll find that the positive has taken over again. Then you are free to proceed."

"What if there is no time for patience? What if I must act urgently?"

"You'll always have time enough for one breath.

One conscious, deep breath. It's surprising how a small surge of oxygen in your body will instantly add more patience and understanding, and transform your negative state into a positive one."

The young boy drew in a deep breath and exclaimed, "Hey, it works! The desire to punch you hard has totally disappeared."

They laughed.

The positive was in control now.

YOU ARE YOUR RESPONSIBILITY

*T*he young boy was pacing the room while biting his nails.

"Hey Chewawa, gonna finish off your nails? What's the matter? Something you want to talk about?" the Universe asked.

"There's lots on my mind. We have an inter-school computer coding competition tomorrow. I am the captain of our team."

"That's wonderful."

"That's not wonderful. I am the captain, the one in charge. I am responsible for what happens to all of us. What if I make a mistake? What if I do something or worse, don't do something needed at the right time? What if I fail the ones who are counting on me? The ones looking at me for guidance and support? What will happen to all of them? I can't let them down. They are under my care, my protection, they are my responsibility. I..."

"Hey, hold it right there," the Universe interrupted. "First, relax. Anxiety helps no one. It only clouds your judgment. Second, I heard you say twice that they are your responsibility. Let me assure you, only 'you' are your responsibility. Others are mine."

"Yours? You are not even on the team!," the young boy protested.

"I am the Universe, ain't I,?" the Universe asked.

The young boy nodded.

"Stop carrying their burden on your shoulders. They are not a burden, to begin with, but all this stress and worrying about it is making it seem so to you. And you'll grow to resent them for that. That imagined weight will make you stoop low. Check your posture. It is not your load to carry. It never was. You are so exhausted trying to care for others; while you are neglecting what is truly your responsibility."

"What's that?," the young boy asked.

"To take care of your own self. Your happiness, peace, and success are yours to choose. And whether others choose their happiness or their lessons is their choice. Most definitely, as their captain; you should lead them, point them in the right direction according to your best judgment."

"Whether they follow your course or set their own path, you can choose to respect their journey. You may be on the same team, walking hand in hand on the same path for the moment, but everyone has their own unique destinations. Their map is safely locked away in their own hearts. The way is revealed to everyone, one step at a time. Follow that invisible map, and it will lead you all home, safe and sound."

"But if you get too bothered about others, you'll lose your own way. That can't be cool, right?" the Universe asked.

"Nope."

"So take responsibility for your own self. Set your mind right before you begin anything. And trust that the outcome will be best for all concerned."

"Cool, on it. By the way, I hope you won't forget your responsibility of getting us an after competition Pizza, right?"

The Universe smiled and said, "Papa John's, I remember."

LAZYBONES

"Where do you get all your answers from?" the young boy asked.

"The same place where you get all your questions from," the Universe replied. "If you look at your questions deep enough, you'll find the answers too, without the need to ask me."

"Lazybones!" the young boy said, punching the Universe.

DROP MIC

"*D*oes it all end in death?" the young boy asked.

"What do you do with your old clothes?" the Universe asked. "The ones too worn out, or the ones you are bored with, or the ones too small for you since you have grown?"

"Donate them or discard them."

"And?"

"Get new ones."

"Exactly," the Universe replied and dropped the Karaoke mic.

The young boy smiled.

THE ONE PERCENTER

"*I* just found out that less than 1% of the world's population makes over $1 Million in a year. Why do you think the other 99% don't deserve to be millionaires?" the young boy asked.

"It's not a question of why I think they don't deserve to be millionaires. It's a question of why 'they' don't believe they deserve to be millionaires. The only two differences between those 1 percenters and the rest 99 percenters are beliefs, and actions based on those beliefs," the Universe replied.

"I believe." the young boy said, steel in his voice. "Now help me choose my Merc."

The Universe smiled and set the wheels in motion.

YOUR TRUE NATURE

"Why does life sometimes feel like a struggle?" the young boy asked.

"That's because you are going against your true nature," the Universe replied.

"Your life is unfolding perfectly, but you have a problem with it because you have a certain perception that things have to be a certain way."

"Things don't have to be any other way than they are. Learn to accept them and then chart your way through them accordingly. If you like them, great. If you don't like them, take action to change them."

"You say life feels like struggle... Life is effortless, my friend. A blade of grass grows by itself. It doesn't struggle to grow, it just grows. Flowers don't try to bloom, they bloom. That doesn't mean they don't face challenges. They have learned to handle the challenges in an effortless way, too. They have been alive for eternity, yet there is no struggle in them. Only an effortless, tranquil beauty."

"Challenges, everyone will have. How you look at them will determine whether you feel struggle or you feel excitement that things are changing. The only thing that makes change hard is that you don't allow it, you fight and resist it. You try to cling to the safety of something that has already started to fade. You look for security in the old and the familiar. True security lies in the wisdom of uncertainty. When you don't know what's going to happen next, that's when the highest possibility for something wonderful truly exists. Besides," the Universe continued with a warm smile on its face, "Why would I give you something you won't be able to handle?"

The young boy felt peace dawning within him. He said, "If a blade of grass can do this, then I got this."

The Universe smiled.

DANCING LIKE MADMEN

"*I* am very, very, very tense," the young boy said, fidgeting on his rocking horse.

"I could have never guessed," the Universe replied with a wink.

The young boy gave him a look.

The Universe shrugged and said, "Fine, I'll bite. Tell me, what's bothering you?"

"I am very, very, very tense about my interview tomorrow. What if I don't get selected?"

"It's a Kindergarten interview... if you show up with a running nose, you'll get selected," the Universe sniggered.

"No way. You don't understand; things are very different now. They can be very strict. And they ask you questions and test you even before they have taught you... Such a scam, I tell you."

The Universe laughed its guts out.

"You are not helping!," the young boy snapped.

"Okay, okay..." the Universe said, controlling the laughter, "let's do something that'll help you."

"What?"

"First, tell me, have you prepared for tomorrow? Memorised days of the week, your address, parents' full names, etc.?"

"Yes."

"And have you done your best to be ready for tomorrow? Your absolute best to get selected?"

"Yes."

"Then why are you nervous?"

"I am nervous because it hasn't happened yet... what if I make a mistake? Things could go either way."

"Ah, I see. Doubt and fear. Well, there's only one solution to that."

"What?" the young boy asked.

"When you have done all you can, to have what you want, there's only one thing left. Positive Expectation. The calm and detached feeling of looking forward to a successful outcome; even before you do it. You need to have a positive expectation of it on a mental, physical, emotional and spiritual level even before taking action. When you have set your mind right thus you are ready for the action."

"So how do I set my mind right? How do I get into that emotional, mental, and all the other levels you spoke about, and have a positive expectation?"

"By celebrating the positive outcome before it happens."

"Celebrating before it happens?"

"That's the best time to celebrate."

"And then, it will happen?"

"You significantly put the odds in your favour. When you celebrate physically, your emotions will change to happy ones. That will lead to happy thoughts. That happiness will go right to your heart and spirit. And happy emotions = happy outcomes."

The young boy's face lit up. The worry lines had long left it. Jumping off his horse he said, "Let's celebrate with cookies and dancing like madmen."

The Universe smiled and kicked off its shoes.

The music and laughter flowed through the neighbourhood, and the happy emotions rippled across the Milky Way.

YOU ARE AN EARTHWORM

"*W*ho am I?" the young boy asked.

"An Earthworm," replied the Universe.

"Eeeww...! Why an earthworm? They are so gross!"

"Well then, you must be gross."

"No way! Why do you say I am an Earthworm? Don't I look so different?"

"And that makes you different, is it?" the Universe.

"Doesn't it?"

"Earthworms, just like everything else on this planet; the trees, the fish, animals, human beings, birds; all of them call this Earth their home, right?"

"Right."

"And what do you call the ones who live in a home

together?"

"A family?"

"Correct. And a family is made of individuals who relate to each other. And it has its differences and fights, but ultimately, deep in its heart, it is true to its roots. Those bonds run deep. That's why you'll find people living miles or hearts apart, but they will forever keep relating to each other. They'll carry their families in their hearts in terms of what they want or don't want in their own lives. Estranged siblings or lovers will never forget each other. The bonds that connected them remain forever, whether they accept or deny them."

"Where there was a sense of love and belonging once, in some form, it always remains. The nature and appearance of things may change. But don't let that fool you. The fact is, what was once dear and important, in some form, remains forever."

"Hmm... well, earthworms are cute too."

The Universe smiled, "See when you remember how connected you are, it is so easy to forgive and love everyone... even earthworms."

The young boy smiled with all his heart. And his big, extended family smiled right back at him.

"*W*hy do good things happen to bad people? Why should they get so many nice things and experiences in life? What gives them the right to deprive others of those things?" the young boy asked.

"And who decided they are bad people?" the Universe asked.

"Isn't it obvious? Duh!"

"No, it's not. The game is still on. Please don't be so quick to judge them or the situation too. It's good, it's bad, it's relative. When all's done and settled, you'll see that it was all good after all."

"And there is no such thing as depriving anyone of anything. There is nothing in this whole wide world that is not infinite. Things are only limited by your imagination, and your capacity to love."

"So stop judging people. Once you learn to love them with no judgments, you'll not only discover the good in people; you will also bring it out in the sun. The world could sure use more of that... The goodness of people's hearts manifested out here in the world. Imagine what a wonderful world that would be."

The Universe was smiling serenely, lost in the beauty of the thought.

The young boy imagined.

And it was so.

WILD AND FREE

"*Y*ou wouldn't believe what happened today!" the young boy's face was lit up with excitement.

"You saw horses?!" the Universe replied.

"How did you know?"

"You are just back from your friend's house, and he owns a stable. Duh!"

"You know everything Universe!" the young boy said, grinning. "Anyway, the horses were majestic. They are famous racehorses, you know. Muscles rippling through their long legs, coats shining, and hair brushed to perfection, I just loved them. I think it was one of the finest stables ever. They treated the horses like royalty. Great caretakers, round-the-clock service, etc."

"So the horses must be happy?" the Universe asked.

"Hmm... Now that you ask, I was so excited when some of them let me pet them, touch their nose and forehead. I got to look into their eyes. Here they were, getting the best treatment ever, more care and attention bestowed upon them than any other horse on the planet. And yet, I saw sadness in their eyes. I can't explain it, but it was there."

"So the stable they were in, what was it like?," the Universe prodded.

"It was impressive. Air-conditioned, lots of organic grass and feed.. many attendants and individual water tanks. Each of the horses had a wonderful concrete cubicle with a door with bars low enough so I could reach up and touch them."

"And the door was open?"

"No, they locked it, of course. They don't want the horses to be wandering around."

"So the horses couldn't go out for a walk if they so wanted?"

"No, they are thoroughbred, my friend's dad told me. Some perform at shows even. They are worth millions, almost like film stars amongst horses."

"And yet, they are confined to their concrete

cubicles, and can't even go out for a walk when they want."

"That's true."

"That's the thing, buddy. Horses in your story are just like human spirits. You can't confine them and expect them to be happy. However pampered they may be, horses are not made to be pampered. They are meant to run wild. Drink from flowing rivers and streams, eat wild grass and make their lives on their terms."

"Similarly, the human spirit is not meant to be locked away in the confines of oppression, fear or expectation. It was made to be free, to soar the skies, to do what its highest desire is. Let loose a horse in the wild and see if it ever craves the comforts of a confined stable, no matter how royal."

"Let your spirit free and see if it ever chooses the shackles of fear again. Sometimes the temptations may be strong, but fear is not your true nature. Fear is a protection device, a survival mechanism. It has a useful purpose. It helps you in avoiding danger and not dying. But it doesn't help you live. Not dying and living are two different things. Any prison, even the one made of your thoughts, fears or beliefs will put the same sadness in your eyes you saw in the stables."

"Whenever you notice that sadness reflected in the mirror a few days in a row, ask yourself - where is my spirit locked away? What chains have I put on it?"

"Because while other people have forged those chains with their disempowering beliefs; you have chained your spirit with them by your own hands, and with your consent."

"The upside is, since you have put those chains on, you can drop them just as easily, in an instant, when you become aware of them and want to reclaim your spirit. It requires faith and action on your part to break those chains."

"And when, once again, you are running in the wild, and stop over for a drink from a fresh rainwater pond, you'll see the face of adventure and life pulsating in your eyes. That light in your eyes will help others drop their chains and be free of their limitations too," the Universe replied.

The light was burning bright in the young boy's eyes by now. He vowed to take this light to millions across the world.

Soon after, he did it.

On his travels, whenever he stopped for a drink, he checked his reflection to make sure that his spirit was wild and free. In the water, beside him, he could always see the face of a dear friend, the Universe, smiling at him, pride, love and a hint of mischief beaming in its eyes.

THE FUN CONTINUES

Read ALL the books in the series.

A Young Boy and His Best Friend, The Universe Vol. I

A Young Boy and His Best Friend, The Universe, Vol. II

A Young Boy and His Best Friend, The Universe, Vol. III

A Young Boy and His Best Friend, The Universe, Vol. VII

Don't miss out on any of the fun adventures of

these two beloved characters. These books can be read and enjoyed in any order.

Connect with the author at:

www.ChannelingHigherWisdom.com

ACKNOWLEDGMENTS

I owe great love and gratitude to my dear family. I live an almost nomadic life, calling different cities my home every few years, stubbornly refusing to 'settle down'. But my family keeps me firmly anchored.

My super-awesome, super-smart, gorgeous sister, Dr Monica Talur. She's such a powerful woman, full of energy, charisma and boundless love for her family and friends alike. She makes me feel like the luckiest brother in the world. Wishing you tons of love and blessings from the Universe that you deserve, Sis.

My nephew, Hriday. At such a tender age, he builds websites by writing thousands of lines of code, earns his right as a World Record holder in Minecraft, and calms people around him with such understanding and love; and even beats me at chess without thinking. Thanks for this blessing, Universe.

My brother-in-law, Dr Narahari Talur, who is such a caring, loving son, husband, and father. A loyal friend of his dear friends and a loving elder brother to his younger siblings. A more devoted son will be hard to find.

To my father, Pramod Dattu Kochure. Dad came from extremely humble beginnings, encountered more than his fair share of challenges and, even on crutches, stood like a mountain behind his family. Sending you love and gratitude, Pappa.

My favourite aunt, Viju maushi, and Tayade uncle. They have been second parents to Sis and me. And they make such an adorable couple. Maushi's love is only matched by uncle's maturity.

My cousins, Sam, Pinks, and Gau. The three of them are such unique personalities, and yet united in their devotion to parents and their love for us. Feel so happy to be with them.

My second nephew, Ishaan. The little genius who reads General Knowledge and aces Olympiad exams at an age where I would use the abbreviation GK because I wasn't sure I would get the spelling of General Knowledge right. Such a joy being with him.

Dear reader, I would like to take a moment here to

thank you for your patience with my lengthy family dedications. In my earlier volumes, I had wrapped them up briefly, out of fear of boring you. But I have grown in this journey of channeling my books and realised something very important. However much we love and respect our family, we rarely openly express how much we love them and how much they mean to us.

And yet, not even a single more second on this planet is guaranteed to us. So why keep that love locked away in our hearts? I strongly urge you to put this book down right now and tell someone how much they mean to you. Trust me, looking a little goofy and feeling a little awkward doing so, is way better than the regret of never having fully expressed how someone meant the world to you. So what if they already know, they would love to hear it again. Trust me. And so what if they don't share your feelings? True love expects nothing in return. It only matters that you loved. So share your love.

Moving on.

In the process of channeling my books and helping the wisdom of the Universe reach you, I have realised few essential truths. This journey has provided ample proof that you can't help someone without being helped yourself.

While the deadline for this book was approaching, I was increasingly getting anxious. I didn't know if I would meet it and started rushing. At one point, I suspected that my anxiety for the book's success had got the better of me, and 2/3 chapters I wrote then didn't feel channeled. Luckily, I was drawn to two books in my library. One by Shakti Gawain and the other by Linda Goodman. Both shared a similar sentiment about work. Linda said, and I paraphrase, 'Do the work that you would do, even if you were paid no money for it at all. Do it because you love it and you simply can't help doing it. Then it will become a labour of love. The highest form of work you can do. It'll bring you inner fulfilment and outward success.'

Reading that took away all my anxiety. This book started flowing gently, like a river. And it has now found its way to you. Never underestimate the power of books to transform your life. Turn to them often, especially when stuck, and the priceless wisdom of the ages will surely guide you.

Sending you love and gratitude for your divine guidance, Shakti Gawain and Linda Goodman.

Next, I would like to thank Shifu Carlton Hill, my Tai Chi teacher. I am learning from him how 'i' am nothing. In the past, I used to make such a big deal about 'me,' 'mine,' 'I did it,' etc. but the truth is I am nobody. Alone, I have done nothing and never will. I am just an instrument for the energy of the Universe. I feel blessed the Universe chose me to be a channel to get its message to you.

The medium is not important, just the message.

Burt Goldman, Jose Silva, and Dr Bimol Rakshit. It was right after a meditation by Burt Goldman that I was guided to write this book series. I am a better person for having written it. And the books are helping people across the world in their humble way. So, much gratitude goes to these humanitarians.

Tejal Mamaniya, a dear friend and spiritual guide, who shares her birthday with my Mom. I was hesitating to commit to a deadline for this book because I struggled to meet my last book's timeline. It felt like work, not a labour of love.

She insisted and set a launch date for this book. And, together with Shakti and Linda, taught me to work with love, towards a definite timeline. What a wonderful way to work, not worrying about success, but just expressing your love through your work. Finishing this book from that space has been such a peaceful, serene experience.

No anxiety, only tranquillity.

I would also like to express my heartfelt gratitude to Surendran Jayasekar. I approached him when I was struggling to finish my second book. Running multiple businesses successfully, and transforming people's lives across India, he's a very busy man. But he was available for me at my first call for help. I asked him to be my commitment partner, and he immediately agreed. I raised the stakes of my commitment to my book deadlines by asking him for a few things I wanted from him, which he would have given me just like that, out of the graciousness of his heart. However, I asked him to only give them to me if I achieved my deadlines and kept my end of the bargain. He agreed, and that renewed my energy. Thanks to him, I could meet the seemingly impossible deadline for my next two books, because the stakes were so high. Thanks for helping me be on track Suren.

To Eberhard Grossgasteiger, for giving me the permission to use his beautiful photographs for the cover art of my books.

To Ahsan Ali, for his love of film and making me look awesome in the author photograph.

Next, perhaps the most important dedication.

I dedicate this book to you, my dear reader. You are the reason these adventures were channeled through me. These books only exist to serve you.

Lastly, to my best friend for eternity, the Universe.

I would still be walking around looking serious, if it weren't for you buddy. Big love to you.

Let's dance this happy dance together, forever.

With love and gratitude,
Sameer Kochure.

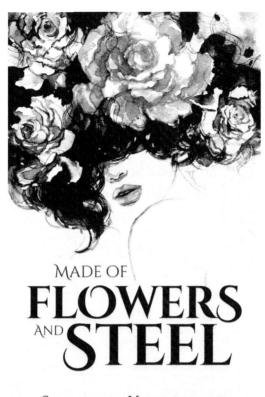

MADE OF
FLOWERS
AND STEEL

SAMEER KOCHURE

**Welcome to a poetry collection that
celebrates the strength behind the beauty
that is a woman.**

*I*nspired by stories of real women, **this
collection of 100 poems honours
the raw grit and the moral fortitude that**

exists in all women. Sometimes that power is inherent, sometimes it needs to be invoked, but it is always there.

Page after page, you'll discover a newfound love and respect for yourself, and for all the women in your life.

Written by Sameer Kochure, the author of the much adored book series *'A Young Boy and His Best Friend, The Universe,'* and *'Wrong. - An inspirational poetry collection,'* this is an easy to read, yet strikingly powerful work of art.

This is NOT a regular book of poems on love, heartbreak or feminism. **It's a salute to the moral strength it takes to be a woman** in today's world. The steel beneath the flowers.

An empowering and a comfort read for all the thinking, feeling women around the world, and for everyone who loves them.

100 Poems | 1 Unmissable Collection

BUY NOW

ALSO BY SAMEER KOCHURE

The Good Universe Series:

A Young Boy and His Best Friend, The Universe Vol. I

A Young Boy and His Best Friend, The Universe, Vol. II

A Young Boy and His Best Friend, The Universe, Vol. III

A Young Boy and His Best Friend, The Universe, Vol. VII

The 1 Verse Poetry Collection:

Made of Flowers and Steel

Wrong - An Inspirational Poetry Collection

www.ChannelingHigherWisdom.com

Wrong. An Inspirational Poetry Collection

Get a FREE copy of Sameer Kochure's new book at:
www.ChannelingHigherWisdom.com

About the Book:

NASA's Voyager 1 has captured a strange, rhythmic, humming sound vibrating in interstellar space.

Could it be the Universe speaking to us in poetry?

Thus begins this powerful inspirational poetry collection by Sameer Kochure, author of the much adored book series 'A Young Boy And His Best Friend, The Universe.'

Just like that beloved spiritual fable, *this book is full of wisdom shorts that'll help you live a more wholesome life.*

It takes *the inner eye, a thinking heart and a feeling mind,* to appreciate all the beauty that surrounds us. There's just so much of it out there, and the loving Universe that it is; it feeds it to us in small, right-sized portions, the ones we can truly love and appreciate.

No wonder, we keep coming back for more.

Wrong. by Sameer Kochure, FREE Download at www.ChannelingHigherWisdom.com

AN APPEAL

I can live for two months on a good compliment. - Mark Twain.

You have just read a book by an independent author. I hope you enjoyed it. May I request you to share an honest review on your favourite online bookstore and your social media? It will help other readers discover this book and perhaps put a smile on their face. Our world would be so much richer with a few more smiles. If you decide not to share your review, I understand that too. You are already doing a lot for me by simply buying my books, and for that I am eternally grateful. - Sameer Kochure.

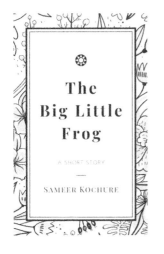

Get a free short story - **The Big Little Frog** as a welcome hug for signing up for my newsletter. The story is a powerful allegory about the consequences of our choices. It's a short read with a big payoff, told with lyrical charm. You'll enjoy it.

Read it at: www.ChannelingHigherWisdom.com

ABOUT THE AUTHOR

Author photo by Ahsan Ali

Sameer Kochure was born in India during the darkest part of the night. Probably explains why he is such a self-proclaimed dreamer. He has lived in 6 cities and 3 countries since. He has also clocked in 12 years as a Creative Director in some of the biggest advertising agencies across Asia Pacific. He lives in

Dubai, but claims that anywhere he travels, he feels he is home.

You can follow Sameer on the following social channels and join his VIP mailing list at:

www.ChannelingHigherWisdom.com

BUY OR BORROW

Libraries played a big part in nurturing my love for reading while growing up. So to give back some of the love libraries have shown me, I have made sure that all my books are easily accessible to major libraries across the world. In case, you don't find any of my books that you want at your library, just fill out a simple book request form, all libraries have them, and more often than not, they will be happy to procure my books for you and honour your request. They love supporting loyal readers like you. Libraries are awesome that way. Show them some love as well. :)

GRATITUDE

Thank you for reading.

You are a true friend of the Universe.

Printed in Great Britain
by Amazon

84376277R00185